LOOSE BULL

Frank and Joe took their seats in the stands as Buck, riding a mean-looking bull, exploded out of a chute. Joe leaned forward to watch the death-defying ride.

The bull launched itself at the cloudless sky, swinging its hind quarters four feet into the air. Joe watched Buck hang on as if he were riveted to the bull's back. "Awesome!" Joe cried. "Now I know why Buck's the best!"

The next moment Buck shuddered strangely, and his hat fell from his hand. Then he slumped forward and was tossed to the ground.

"What's happening?" Joe asked, grabbing Frank's shoulder.

"I don't know but—" Frank stopped when he saw the bull spin around, its horns glinting. It lowered its head to gore the unmoving figure sprawled in the middle of the arena.

"Come on, Joe!" Frank shouted. "We've got to get that bull away from Buck!"

Books in THE HARDY BOYS CASEFILES® Series

Available from ARCHWAY Paperbacks

THE HARDY BOYS CASEFILES NO. 68

ROUGH RIDING

FRANKLIN W. DIXON

AN ARCHWAY PAPERBACK
Published by POCKET BOOKS

New York   London   Toronto   Sydney   Tokyo   Singapore

AN ARCHWAY PAPERBACK *Original*

 An Archway Paperback published by
POCKET BOOKS, a division of Simon & Schuster Inc.
1230 Avenue of the Americas, New York, NY 10020

Copyright © 1992 by Simon & Schuster Inc.
Produced by Mega-Books of New York, Inc.

ISBN: 0-671-73104-1

First Archway Paperback printing October 1992

10 9 8 7 6 5 4 3 2 1

THE HARDY BOYS, AN ARCHWAY PAPERBACK
and colophon are registered trademarks of Simon & Schuster Inc.

THE HARDY BOYS CASEFILES is a trademark
of Simon & Schuster Inc.

Cover art by Brian Kotzky

Printed in the U.S.A.

IL 6+

Chapter

1

"WE'VE NEVER SEEN anything like this back in Bayport!" Joe Hardy shouted, forgetting for a moment that he was in a closed car traveling down a Texas highway.

Beside the road a coal black quarter horse galloped at top speed. The rider sat tall in the saddle, wearing a sweat-stained cowboy hat tugged low over his eyes. Ten feet ahead of the horse a rusty brown calf was running hard, covering ground like a runaway freight train.

Frank Hardy, eighteen and a year older than his brother, Joe, leaned across the rear seat toward the window on Joe's side. He watched as the cowboy whirled a lasso over his head several times and fired the loop at the fast-running calf. It settled perfectly over the animal's head.

1

"Why don't I stop, so you boys and your aunt Gertrude can see what happens next," Viola Halloran said, glancing back at the boys from the driver's seat of the late model station wagon.

A middle-aged woman with a mane of beautiful white hair, Mrs. Halloran was the girlhood friend of Gertrude Hardy, the Hardys' aunt who sat in the front passenger seat. Viola Halloran had just picked them up at the airport outside the town of Dry Valley, Texas.

Gertrude held up her new mini camcorder, which was strapped securely to the palm of her hand. "This will be a great opening for my travelogue about Texas." She rolled down her window and put her eye to the viewfinder.

Viola Halloran braked and pulled onto the shoulder just as the cowboy reined his horse to a sliding stop barely a hundred feet away. As the calf hit the end of the rope, it flipped into the air and slammed to the ground.

"The calf doesn't seem to be enjoying this much," Frank commented.

"Watch and see what happens next," Mrs. Halloran cautioned.

By the time the calf had struggled to its feet, the cowboy was off his horse and kneeling in the dust next to the frightened animal. Frank and Joe watched as he stroked it gently. He seemed to be examining the calf.

"He's checking it over to see if the animal's healthy," Viola told them. "If it shows any sign of sickness, he'll take it back to the ranch for a veterinarian to treat."

"I guess he's satisfied," Joe said, watching the cowboy slip his rope from the calf's neck and send it off with a slap on its backside. The animal shambled away, none the worse for wear. Viola Halloran pulled back onto the highway.

"I'm sure glad I bought some western gear before we got here," Joe said, the brim of the western hat low over his eyes just as the cowboy had worn his. Joe's blond hair stuck out from under the hat like bits of yellow fringe. "I could get into being a cowboy."

"Yeah, with your city-slicker gear bought in a Bayport store," Frank said, and laughed. He was wearing a white polo shirt and jeans.

"It's from a genuine western store," Joe insisted, buffing one of his brand-new, highly polished cowboy boots against his pant leg.

"I'm glad you boys could come out to visit for a couple of weeks—especially these two weeks," Mrs. Halloran said, glancing at the Hardys in the rearview mirror as she drove. "I'm just sorry your parents couldn't come."

"Dad's working on a case," Joe said with pride. Fenton Hardy was a private detective with an international reputation.

"I'm told you two are good sleuths, too," Viola continued.

Frank and Joe exchanged glances. "We help out when we can," Frank said modestly.

3

Aunt Gertrude, who had been videotaping the passing scenery outside the car, set the camcorder in her lap. "Help out, my foot," she snapped. "You two always get involved in your father's most dangerous cases, and some day, if you're not careful—"

"But we are careful," Joe protested. Aunt Gertrude was a worrier and drove Frank and Joe half crazy with her worrying.

"Well, you won't have any crimes out here in Dry Valley," Viola Halloran said with a smile. "You're on vacation, and other than our rodeo, which my son Matt is managing, there's not much going on. Certainly nothing mysterious. Matt is looking forward to meeting you, by the way."

Just then Frank saw a huge billboard ahead on the side of the highway. On it was a cowboy on a bucking horse.

"What are those buildings coming up on the right?" he asked, gazing past the immense billboard. He could make out a small arena surrounded by a high concrete wall. Beside it was a huge barn.

"That's the Dry Valley Rodeo grounds," Viola Halloran said. "This is the fifteenth year that we at the Double X have hosted the rodeo. My husband built the arena and dance hall on our land and was the director until he passed on last year. Now Matt's running the show."

Frank and Joe could now read the words

4

below the cowboy and bucking horse: Famous Rodeo Stars Cowboy Buck and Rodeo Rick In Action!

"Fantastic!" Joe exclaimed. "I read about Cowboy Buck Fuller in a magazine last month. Rodeo Rick was the biggest rodeo champion until Buck hit the scene. In barely two years he's risen right to the top."

"That's right," Viola said. "Thanks to Buck's coming here, all the tickets are already sold out. Folks from miles around will get to see him ride bulls and horses."

"Sounds like a major responsibility for Matt, Mrs. Halloran," Frank observed. "It must be hard to put everything together."

"It's our family business," Mrs. Halloran explained. "It's time Matt got his chance to run it."

"Will we get to meet Cowboy Buck Fuller?" Joe asked.

Mrs. Halloran laughed. "I'm sure you will. Not only is he the greatest rodeo star to come along in years, he's also a wonderful person. He devotes much of his time and money to helping poor kids. He'll often drive all night to visit a children's hospital or to make an appearance at a boys' club."

"He sounds like a great guy," Joe said. The car was now passing the rodeo grounds and he noted the rows of cinder block stalls with corrugated tin roofs. Many of the stalls had horses in

5

them, and cowboys in jeans and white straw hats strode through the corrals. Next to the corrals was a field of RVs and campers.

He was about to ask Mrs. Halloran another question about Buck when he saw something that made him forget the famous rodeo rider.

"Hey—wow! Who's that?" He turned in his seat to get a better look as the car moved past a pretty dark-haired girl on a white horse. She was racing across a field, twirling a lasso over her head.

"*She's* part of the Wild West I'd like to get to know!" Joe exclaimed.

Frank laughed. "You wouldn't want to two-time all your girlfriends back home, would you?"

"I'd be tempted," Joe said, watching through the rear window as the girl on the horse grew smaller.

"That's Terri Garcia," Mrs. Halloran told them. "She's a trick roper who entertains the audience between rides. I'm sure you'll get to meet her, too. Matt and Terri are good friends."

Half a mile past the rodeo grounds, Mrs. Halloran turned the car onto a narrow road that ran between long rows of tall cottonwood trees and white corral fences. "Welcome to the Double X," she said.

The road continued another half mile to three huge barns and a large, two-story redbrick house. Mrs. Halloran pulled the car to a stop in front of the house.

"Is this a working ranch?" Joe asked. "I mean, do you raise cattle."

"We stopped after my husband built the rodeo grounds," she explained. "The town of Dry Valley had started spreading out this way, so we sold some of our land to a developer to raise money for the rodeo. After that we concentrated on breeding horses and running the rodeo."

Just as the Hardys climbed out of the station wagon, Joe noticed a young man on a spotted horse galloping toward them across a field that bordered the house. He urged the horse up, and together they leapt the fence to land on the driveway. He was wearing a Stetson hat and leather chaps over his blue jeans.

"That's my son, Matt," Mrs. Halloran said proudly, waving to him. The rider reined in his horse and trotted toward them. Aunt Gertrude had her camcorder glued to her eye the entire time. After she zoomed in on Matt and the horse, she started panning the entire ranch.

Joe laughed. "It's impossible to get everything on tape, you know."

"Aunt Gertrude, I hope you take some time off from taping to enjoy your vacation," Frank commented.

The boys' aunt lowered the camera and narrowed her eyes at them. "This *is* how I'm enjoying my vacation," she told him. "And I'm sure when we get back to Bayport, you and Joe will be very happy to see yourselves on tape."

Matt Halloran reined his horse up next to the car and swung his leg over the saddle to dismount. He was a tall, handsome young man with inky black hair and brown eyes. As Mrs. Halloran introduced him, he shook Frank's hand first. His grip was friendly and strong. When he shook hands with Joe, he smiled slowly and said, "I see you've stocked up on western duds, Joe."

"You got that right," Joe said. "I want to fit right in. Maybe I'll even enter and win a few events at the rodeo!" he kidded.

"Not with Buck Fuller entered." Matt laughed. "Rodeo Rick is here, too, and he's a top hand."

"Top hand?" Frank asked.

"A guy who's the best in a rodeo event like roping or riding broncs or bulls," Matt explained. "Maybe you guys would like to meet some of the competitors. They're here from all over the Southwest."

"I'd like to meet Buck Fuller and—"

"Terri Garcia," Joe added, interrupting his brother.

Matt and Frank broke out in laughter. "I can understand why you'd want to meet Terri," Matt teased. "She is pretty—and she happens to be the best trick roper in Texas."

Mrs. Halloran took Aunt Gertrude's arm. "Come on, Gert," she said. "Let's leave the boys to get acquainted and go inside. I'll show you your room."

Aunt Gertrude looked around wistfully, fidgeting with her camcorder. "I guess I can do some more videotaping later," she said. She joined Viola Halloran to walk toward the house.

"Beautiful horse," Frank said to Matt, patting the animal's flank. "Do you compete in any of the rodeo events?"

Matt shook his head. "As the director, I'm not eligible. Running a rodeo is a full-time job if you do it right. I'm only twenty-two years old and have to prove myself every step of the way. When my dad first started the rodeo, it was small-time, just a local contest." He waved toward the rodeo grounds, which were visible across the fields about half a mile away. "Today that's what he built it into—"

The thundering of hoofbeats cut Matt off. Frank and Joe spun to face a group of horsemen riding up the long driveway to the house.

"Rodeo Rick," Matt said. "He doesn't look happy. I wonder what's up."

As Frank and Joe watched the riders approach, a tall, thin man with a white Stetson, and the initials *RR* monogrammed on the pocket flap of his western shirt, pulled out in front. He pulled his coal black horse to a stop.

Rodeo Rick slid down from his saddle to stand in front of Matt. He wasn't young; in fact, when he whipped off his hat and ran a forearm across his sweaty brow, Joe could see that his dark brown hair was flecked with gray. His face was red and he looked angry.

"There's a jailbird riding in the Dry Valley Rodeo and we don't like it!" Rick shouted.

"What are you talking about?" Matt asked evenly. "Calm down and tell me what's got you all riled up." The other riders stayed on their horses, intimidating the boys as they circled round them.

Rick continued. "That big-shot Buck did a year in the state pen for car theft. Me and the boys don't want to ride against no criminal." He questioned the other riders. "Right, men?"

The cowboys looked at one another and nodded their agreement. "Rick's right," several said, but they seemed to speak without enthusiasm.

Frank turned to Joe. "I'd say Rodeo Rick is the only one who's all fired up," he told his brother quietly.

Joe nodded. "I wonder why?"

"Where'd you get this information, Rick?" Matt demanded.

"One of the bronc riders was a state trooper before he started on the circuit. He remembered Buck Fuller because he helped arrest him for car theft." Rick moved closer to Matt, until he was practically shouting in the young man's face. Frank was almost afraid the encounter would turn into a brawl.

"Now, what are you going to do about it? Our

overnight hero ain't such a hero after all, is he?"
Rick demanded.

Matt stood his ground. "I'll look into this,
Rick," he said steadily. "But I'll tell you right
now: if Buck did make a mistake earlier in his
life that's his business, not yours or mine."

"Are you saying me and the boys have to ride
against a common criminal?" Rick snarled, not
waiting for an answer. "That's no good for us
and it's no good for the rodeo."

"That's the way it's got to be, Rick," Matt
said grimly. "Buck's a big draw—maybe even
bigger than *you* are," he added quietly.

Frank watched as Rodeo Rick flinched and
turned red. "But—but you can't—"

"Sure I can, Rick," Matt said. "If he's done
his time, we aren't going to hold his past against
him. Buck stays."

Without another word, Rodeo Rick stomped
up to his horse, snatched the reins from his
friend's hand, and swung into the saddle. His
face was set and furious.

"We'll just see about that, Matt," he stated
simply, staring down from his lofty position.
"Because if you don't do something about that
jailbird, I will!"

Chapter

2

FRANK, JOE, AND MATT watched the men gallop off, their horses' hooves throwing clouds of dust high into the hot, west Texas air.

"Rick sure is upset about Buck," Joe said, breaking the silence that surrounded them.

"Yeah, and I don't think the problem is with Buck's past," Frank added.

Matt nodded. "You got that right. Rick is afraid Buck will win this year. Rick's best days are pretty much behind him, and Buck is young and hot. He's won over seventy-five thousand dollars this year, and he's still going strong."

"Wow!" Joe exclaimed. "I didn't know there was that kind of money in rodeo."

"There is if you're good," Matt said. "And Buck is."

"What are you going to do about Rick's accusations?" Frank asked squarely.

Matt sighed. "As director of the Dry Valley Rodeo, I need to know the truth in case I'm ever asked about it. Let's take your bags up to your room and then we'll go over to the rodeo grounds to find Buck."

Frank and Joe hoisted their suitcases out of the back of the station wagon, while Matt grabbed Aunt Gertrude's. The brothers followed him up the steps of the huge, redbrick house and through the white front door. Inside, Frank noted the traditional ranch furnishings. Carved wooden furniture and a huge stone fireplace dominated the living room. A staircase spiraled up to the second floor from the entrance hall. Matt showed the brothers to their room, which had a private bath and a view overlooking fields and the distant rodeo grounds.

A few minutes later Frank and Joe were back outside waiting as Matt drove up in a red sedan with Texas plates that read XX RANCH.

"Most of the time I use a four-wheeler, but I left it at the rodeo grounds and rode back here on horseback," Matt told them. "Mom said for you to feel free to use this car while you're here."

"Great," Joe responded. "Maybe I'll invite Terri Garcia to go for a little moonlight ride some night."

13

"My brother has a one-track mind," Frank said to Matt.

Matt laughed. "I don't blame you for liking Terri," he told Joe. "But I should warn you that she's got a mind of her own."

The drive to the rodeo was short. They entered the grounds through a big, front gate framed by logs. Frank and Joe gazed at the arena with its high concrete walls. A sign across the top spelled out Dry Valley Rodeo in hundreds of lights. Matt parked in a field with pickup trucks and cars. Most of the trucks had horse trailers attached to or next to them.

"The cowboys who do calf roping bring their own horses," Matt explained. "Some of them travel over twenty thousand miles during the rodeo season, going from town to town."

Frank gazed toward a small pen outside the arena. "What's that?" he asked.

"That's where the bulls the cowboys ride are penned," Matt told him. "They have to be kept separate from the bucking horses and the roping calves. Bulls are about the meanest animals on earth. With their weight of more than twelve hundred pounds and those sharp horns, they're really dangerous."

"Aren't the bucking horses dangerous, too?" Frank asked.

"They can be." Matt nodded. "But when a horse dumps a rider, it just runs to the far end

14

of the arena. A bull won't do that. He'll try to stomp and gore a rider who's down."

Joe swallowed hard. "I think I'll stay far away from the bulls," he said.

Two cowboys stepped out of an RV and waved to Matt. Both carried long ropes in their hands. Matt waved back and continued walking. Joe noticed that the two cowboys put their heads together to speak. Then they grinned. Moving faster than Joe could take in, they swung their ropes over their heads. Two wide loops snaked out. One dropped over Frank—the other circled Joe.

"Hey," Joe yelled. "What are you doing!"

The ropers pulled on their ropes, tightening the loops and drawing the Hardys toward them. Frank struggled but soon realized he couldn't begin to move his arms. Laughing hard, the cowboys tossed some slack into their ropes and the loops fell free. Watching, Matt was laughing even harder than the cowboys.

"Frank and Joe, I want you to meet Hank and Boone." He waved the two cowboys over. Hank was tall and as thin as a post. His dark-haired friend was the opposite—short and stocky.

"They're top ropers," Matt said proudly.

"You can't get by without us having some target practice," Hank drawled as the Hardys good-naturedly shook hands.

"I'd sure like to learn some rope tricks," Joe stated. "Is it okay if I watch you practice?"

"Sure," Boone replied. "But we don't do tricks. We only rope calves. Maybe you should talk to Terri Garcia. She knows every rope trick invented."

"And then some," Hank added.

A big smile spread across Joe's face.

Frank nudged his brother. "That's the best advice you've heard in a long time."

Matt Halloran said goodbye to Hank and Boone and led the Hardys around the back of the arena, where Frank stopped short. "What in the world is that?" he asked. He was pointing at a big barrel with a saddle strapped to it that sat on metal arms above a small gasoline engine.

Matt led the Hardys to the strange contraption. "This is what the bull riders use to practice. The motor moves those arms and they make the barrel bounce and jerk around. It's like riding a bucking bull. You guys want to try it?" Matt offered.

"Sure!" Joe answered instantly.

Matt pulled the cord and the motor chugged to life. Joe climbed up on the saddle.

"If you're right-handed, grab that rope in front of the saddle with your right hand and keep your left up in the air. If a cowboy touches a bronc or a bull with his free hand, it's a foul and he gets no points for the ride."

Joe settled himself in the saddle with his arms and hands in the right position.

"Okay, Joe," Matt called. "Here goes!" He

shifted the motor into gear. The engine roared, and the barrel began to spin and leap up and down, seeming to tilt at every angle at the same time.

"Ride 'em, cowboy!" Frank shouted.

Joe felt the vibrations of the mechanical bucking bull pound through his body. He gripped the reins tightly, while his left arm flapped up and down with the motions of the barrel. "There's nothing to this!" he shouted happily.

"Try this then!" Matt shouted over the loud rumble of the motor. He opened the throttle to increase the speed. Joe found himself clenching the reins tighter and gripping the barrel with his legs as hard as he could to stay on.

The speed of the mechanical bull picked up. Suddenly Joe felt his body being jolted back and forth so hard he thought his bones would come right out of their sockets. The knuckles of his right hand were white from clutching the rope. The vibrating barrel unexpectedly dipped and spun at the same time. Before he knew it, Joe was airborne. Instinctively, he curled and rolled to lessen the impact of his fall. The mound of hay that had been piled loosely around the machine also cushioned his fall.

"Good ride," Matt said, giving Joe a hand up. "That was only about quarter speed, though. I think you see that this rodeo stuff takes real skill."

"I sure do!" Joe said, laughing. "Go on, Frank," he urged. "Try it."

Frank rather reluctantly climbed aboard and secured the rope in his right hand. After watching Joe fly through the air, he wasn't eager to ride the machine, but at least he had seen what it could do and prepared himself for the worst.

Matt eased the motor out of neutral again, and the barrel began to spin and dip. Frank gripped his legs tightly around the barrel and held on to the rope, whooping and laughing. Matt increased the speed. Frank felt the machine pitch and turn faster and harder, rocking his body left then right. He held tight, though, and discovered that he could use his outstretched left hand as a kind of rudder in the air.

"Way to go!" Joe yelled enthusiastically. "Show that rig it's got a Hardy on its back!"

Matt increased the speed once more, and the engine now roared like that of a stock car. Frank clenched his teeth, focusing all his strength on hanging on. A moment later the machine won and Frank felt himself sailing through the air to land in a mound of hay the way Joe had.

"That was fun." He laughed and brushed hay from his shirt. "I'd try it again some time."

"Any time," Matt offered. "You both made pretty good rides."

"Only pretty good?" Joe asked.

"I'm afraid so." Matt grinned. "This thing is

only about half as difficult as a real bull or bucking horse."

"And that motor isn't going to chase us down the way you said a bull would," Frank pointed out.

"That's for sure," Matt said. He gestured toward the campground filled with RVs and trailers. "Let's go over and meet Cowboy Buck Fuller. Maybe he'll give you some tips on how to ride the mechanical bull."

Matt led them toward a small RV parked in the shade of a big old cottonwood tree. As the Hardys approached, a man and woman stepped out the door. Unaware that they had visitors, they were talking and smiling at each other.

"That's strange," Matt said quietly to the Hardys. "Buck is with his wife. I thought they split up about a month ago."

He waved at the couple and called out, "Buck and Loretta! I want you to meet friends of mine from out of state. Frank and Joe Hardy." He turned to the brothers. "Frank and Joe, this is Buck Fuller and his wife, Loretta."

Frank shook hands with Buck, noting that the cowboy was about three inches shorter than he was. Buck's brown hair was long, and he had friendly chestnut eyes. His handshake was firm, and the rolled-up sleeves of his western-style shirt showed tight, bulging arm muscles.

Loretta turned to Joe and offered her hand.

"Nice meeting you," she said. "I'm just on

my way to do some practicing, but you stay and visit with Buck.''

Joe shook her hand, finding himself a little tongue-tied in front of such a beautiful woman. Loretta, who was about five feet five, had cornflower blue eyes. She wore her long golden hair in a braid that reached almost to her waist.

"Practicing?" Joe asked. "You don't mean that you ride bulls, too?"

"Heavens no!" Loretta laughed. "They're a little too dangerous for me. I'm a trick shot. I perform between rides at the rodeo."

"Loretta can shoot the whiskers off a fly at a hundred feet," Buck said proudly.

"And she's a local girl, too," Matt added.

"My pa has a ranch called the Flying B outside of Dry Valley," Loretta told the Hardys.

"Frank and Joe are famous private detectives," said Matt.

"Actually, our dad's the famous detective," Frank said coolly, casting a quick glance at Joe.

"We've helped out on a few cases," Joe added modestly.

"You don't say," Buck said. "I hired a private detective to work for me once. Didn't have much luck with what I asked him to find out. Maybe you guys could help me out."

"Sure," Joe said. "Just let us know when."

"Well, you fellows can jaw all you want," Loretta said. She rose up a bit to kiss her husband.

"I've got some practicing to do for the opening day after tomorrow."

As Loretta walked away, Buck turned to Matt. "I guess it's no secret that Loretta and I haven't always gotten along the way a husband and wife should," he said. "We're both kind of hot-tempered, and traveling on the professional rodeo circuit has been tough on both of us. But we're going to try again. This time we've decided to talk more and argue less."

"That's wonderful," Matt said. Then he told Buck about the visit he'd had from Rodeo Rick. "I need to know the real story from you," he said.

Frank and Joe watched Buck shuffle nervously a second before meeting Matt's gaze. "Rick's right," he said steadily. "I've done time. I grew up in orphanages and foster homes and always had a real bad attitude. One night I hot-wired a car to take a girl for a joyride. It turned out she was the daughter of a judge. I was sent to the Central Texas Prison Farm for a year."

Buck paused for a moment. "That's where I learned about rodeo. I've been straight and honest ever since," he said firmly. "And I plan on staying that way."

"Why did you hide your past, Buck?" Matt asked. "You should have at least told me so I'd be ready in case anything like this came up."

Buck lowered his eyes to the ground. "I was

afraid if people knew, I wouldn't be allowed to keep on working with poor and hospitalized youngsters. That's real important to me.''

"I know,'' Matt said warmly. "I'll tell you right now your past isn't going to make any difference to me. If you ever need a reference, you make sure they call *me*. I don't believe in holding a mistake against a man—particularly when he's done as well as you have, Buck.''

"Thanks,'' Buck said, smiling shyly. "Say, maybe Joe and Frank would like to have a look around behind the chutes in the arena, Matt. Some of the bull riders are back there getting their gear ready for tomorrow.''

"Let's go,'' Joe said before Matt or Frank could answer.

Buck smiled happily. "I want you to meet my horse, Rocket, too.''

The four of them set off toward the arena entrance. Buck laughed when Joe told him about his ride on the bucking barrel.

"I trained my horse, Rocket,'' Buck told the Hardys. "You should have seen him buck when I first tried to ride him. I spent more time on the ground than in the saddle until I finally broke him.''

They passed by a long row of cinder block stalls, where cowboys were tending horses, and entered the back of the arena. Frank looked over at a maze of steel chutes facing the ring. Behind it he saw the pen where the bulls were kept. The animals mooed plaintively.

"What's that?" Joe asked suddenly.

Frank stared blankly at Joe. "What?"

"Don't you feel it?" Joe said. "The ground's vibrating."

Suddenly Frank saw a cloud of dust rise above the chutes that led from the bull pen to the arena. He heard Buck shout.

"Look out! A bull's loose and he's charging us!"

Just as Buck said it, Frank saw the huge black bull with sharp ugly horns race through the open chute into the arena. The beast paused, glaring with red coal eyes.

"There's nothing to hide behind!" Frank shouted, casting around for a safe place.

The huge bull spotted the boys. Its horns glinted in the sun as it lowered its head and charged.

Chapter

3

"HEAD FOR THAT GATE!" Buck called out, pointing to the front of the arena where a long wooden fence separated the bleachers from the ring. Frank saw an open gate they could get through—if they made it in time.

He started running, with Matt just ahead of him, and Buck and Joe right behind. With every footstep on the ground, he could feel the bull's hooves pounding the earth. A quick glance over his shoulder told him that the dangerous animal was gaining on them.

Just then Matt's boot struck a small hole in the dirt. Frank watched as he went down face first, hard enough to knock the wind out of him. He grabbed Matt's arm and started to yank him up as Joe and Buck caught up to him.

"Go on!" Matt gasped. "Get out of here, I'll catch up!"

"Not without our help," Joe shouted. He grabbed Matt's other shoulder and helped Frank pull their new friend to his feet. Off to the side Frank saw Buck stop and turn to face the bull. The rodeo star was shouting and waving his arms while moving toward the edge of the ring. He was trying to draw the animal away from the others.

Frank and Joe started running again, with Matt's arms slung over their shoulders. Matt forced himself to run as well as he could. He couldn't hide the obvious pain he was in as he stumbled on an injured right ankle.

The bull thundered closer. Joe glanced back and saw it slow down and turn toward Buck, who was still trying to distract it. For a moment, it seemed to Joe that the beast was considering which target to go after. A split second later the bull lowered its head and charged the boys again, doubling its speed.

"Faster!" Joe cried. "It's coming right at us."

He heard Buck yelling harder and louder as the rodeo star tried desperately to get the bull's attention. Suddenly he saw a white horse flash out from the end of the arena.

"It's Terri Garcia," Joe shouted, glancing back at the trick roper, who was riding across the arena. He saw her gallop directly toward the runaway bull, her lasso twirling over her head with the loop wide open.

The Hardys and Matt picked up speed. They were almost safely at the gate. Joe couldn't stop himself from glancing back at the horsewoman as she raced up next to the bull and made a powerful rope throw. The loop dropped a half stride in front of the charging animal.

"She missed!" Joe cried bitterly.

Matt glanced back. "No, she hasn't—"

Matt hadn't even finished his sentence when the bull stepped into the open loop. Joe watched as Terri pulled her horse to an abrupt stop with a swift pull on her reins. The rope closed around the bull's front legs, dumping the gigantic animal in the dirt.

The Hardys and Matt paused, only a few feet from the gate.

"We're safe now," Matt told them, panting to catch his breath.

Frank and Joe watched as two other riders galloped up to Terri. They lassoed the bull around its thick neck as Buck raced across the arena toward the Hardys and Matt.

"You guys okay?" he asked, worry on his face.

Frank nodded.

"I'm fine," Matt answered with a weak smile. "My ankle's a little sore, but I don't think it's broken or anything."

"What'll they do with the bull now?" Joe

asked as Terri Garcia and the two cowboys dragged the struggling bull back to its pen.

"Check it over for injuries," Matt told him. "Could be that the animal is too skittish for the rodeo."

"How did it escape?" Frank asked quietly.

Matt and Buck both shrugged.

"Let's go over and have a look," Joe suggested.

Matt was able to walk on his foot, but slowly. They got to the chutes just as the bull was being shut back inside its pen. It glared out at the Hardys with angry eyes.

"It could really make a shish kebab out of us with those horns," Frank said, observing the sharp points. He turned at the sound of horse's hooves. Terri Garcia was riding toward them. She stopped and swung down off her white horse.

"That was a close call, Matt," she said. "How did that bull get out?"

"I don't know, but I plan to find out," Matt answered.

Frank crouched next to the gate of the animal's pen. "This is a gravity latch," he explained. "The kind that falls down and locks as soon as the gate is shut. This kind of lock is foolproof." He stared up at the others with an expression of concern in his eyes. "It's working just fine now."

Joe noticed Terri staring at Frank. He couldn't

take his eyes off her himself. She was almost his height and had dark eyes that looked deep enough to fall into. Her long, silky black hair complemented her rich brown skin. Since no one seemed about to make introductions, Joe decided to do it himself.

"Er, I'm Joe Hardy," he said, extending his hand. "I'm visiting here from—"

"Oh! I'm sorry," Matt said, and laughed. "Terri, meet Frank and Joe Hardy. They're staying at the Double X for the rodeo."

Terri shook Joe's hand and gave him a quick smile. Then she shook Frank's, but this time she didn't let go.

"It's great to meet you," she said, smiling at Frank. "Where are you from?"

"A little city called Bayport." Frank grinned shyly. Terri was still holding his hand. "Back east. A long way from Texas."

He pulled his hand away from Terri's and pointed to the gravity lock on the gate to the bull pen. "It looks as if somebody opened this," he said. "Maybe the bull was let out on purpose."

"Why would anyone do that?" Terri asked, not taking her eyes off Frank.

"No way," Buck scoffed. "It was an accident. Maybe the bull nudged it somehow, or maybe it just wasn't closed properly."

"Well, maybe," Frank said doubtfully. "But it doesn't make sense."

Joe tore himself away from gazing at Terri Garcia. "The timing was pretty odd," he pointed out to Matt and Buck. "It got out just as we were in the open and a long way from cover."

"Accidents happen," Buck insisted. "Let's forget about it. Right, Matt?"

Matt nodded slowly, his brow furrowed. Frank could tell he was troubled by the incident. "I suppose so, Buck," Matt finally said. "But I have to agree with Frank. It seems fishy to me."

Buck smiled broadly. "Let's pretend it never happened," he suggested. "I don't know about you, but my mouth is pretty dry from all that running around. Why don't you come on over to my RV for a cold bottle of soda pop."

"How about joining us," Joe said to Terri. Frank saw his brother's eyes light up when Terri agreed. He also noticed that the trick roper was looking at him, Frank, all the time.

They traced their steps back to Buck's RV, with Terry Garcia leading her white horse. Buck passed out cans of soda pop, and the small party sat in lawn chairs, shaded by the branches of the old cottonwood tree.

"Terri," Joe began, trying to engage her in conversation, despite the fact that she was obviously interested in Frank. "I'd really like to learn to rope. Do you think you could give me some pointers?"

"I've got a better idea," Terri answered, her eyes drifting over to Frank once again. "I'll teach Frank, and he can teach you when you're back in Baytown."

Frank coughed and felt himself blushing. Unlike Joe, Frank had a steady girlfriend.

"Bay*port,*" Joe corrected Terri politely. He was more than a little taken aback by the trick roper's brush-off. Usually girls vied for his attention. He decided to try again.

"Actually, I think I'd learn better if *you* were my teacher," he said hopefully.

Terri set down her empty can of soda pop. "I've got to brush and groom my horse," she announced, standing. She said goodbye to Matt, Buck, and Joe. When it came to Frank's turn, she smiled and said, "See you around?" It was a question more than a farewell.

Once again Frank blushed. "Uh, sure, Terri." He gestured at Joe. "My brother and I are here for a couple of weeks. Maybe the three of us can get together."

"I'd like that," Terri said.

After she left, the Hardys piled into the red car. Matt drove his four-wheeler back to the Double X. Aunt Gertrude was standing on the front porch, armed with her camcorder as they pulled up. She taped her nephews as they left the car.

"This is a great shot," she told them, "with the barns and pastures behind you. Now I hope you two are careful while we're here in Texas.

There's just no telling when one of these horses or cows could get loose and hurt you."

"They're not cows, Aunt Gertrude," Joe corrected. "They're bulls."

Frank shot Joe a warning not to tell their aunt Gertrude about their close call with the bull. Joe nodded his understanding.

"Well, whatever they are they might be dangerous," Aunt Gertrude said again, finally lowering her video camera. "Viola tells me dinner is in an hour. Don't be late."

Frank and Joe wandered around the Double X to check the ranch out. Since the Hallorans no longer kept cattle, the barn held only a half dozen horses. A crusty old cowhand named Ernie poured oats into the animals' feeding troughs. He explained that the horses were the pride of the Double X and were used for breeding stock.

That night Viola Halloran served an enormous country dinner of steak, potatoes, and salad, topped off with homemade apple pie. After finishing a second piece of pie, Joe pushed his chair back from the table and folded his napkin.

"I'm exhausted," he announced. "It must be all this country air."

"Either that or your second piece of pie," Frank teased.

"You're not taking Terri Garcia out for a moonlight ride?" Matt asked with a big grin.

"Just give me time," Joe assured him confidently.

The next morning Frank and Joe were up by five. The house was quiet, but when they went downstairs they found Mrs. Halloran already in the kitchen, frying up a big breakfast of bacon and eggs.

"For more than twenty years when the Double X was a working ranch I cooked breakfast for a dozen cowboys every morning," she told the Hardys. "So it's no trouble to feed a few hungry guests."

A few minutes later Matt joined them. Soon the three plates of bacon, eggs, and home fries were history.

"I'm riding over to the rodeo grounds," Matt told the brothers after breakfast. "The red car is in the garage behind the house. You guys come over as soon as you want. I'll show you some really fine horses. Rodeo cowboys take better care of their horses than they do themselves." He laughed. "I've known cowboys who'll spend their last dollar on feed for their horses and go hungry themselves."

After Matt rode away from the barn on a large spotted horse, the Hardys walked to the garage where the car was parked. Joe let out his belt a notch on the way.

"If I keep eating like this," he said, "I'll look like a whale by the time the rodeo is over."

"Me, too," Frank agreed. "It's barely seven and I've already eaten more food than I would in a full day back home. We should do something to work off these big meals."

"Like running from bulls, maybe?" Joe joked.

Frank slid behind the wheel of the car and Joe got into the passenger's seat.

"I was thinking about that gate and latch last night just before I dozed off," Frank said, turning the key. "I'm still real suspicious about how that whole thing happened."

Joe studied him curiously. "But why would anyone want to hurt us?"

"I doubt that we were the target," Frank told him. "Remember how mad Rodeo Rick and some of those other men were yesterday? It would have been Buck they wanted to hurt."

Joe nodded. "You could be right. Maybe Rick wants to put Buck out of commission so he won't have so much competition."

Frank shifted the car into reverse and backed out of the garage. He swung the car around and headed down the long drive to the main road. "I think we better keep our eyes open extra wide."

"Right," Joe agreed. "If Buck got hurt, it would really be bad for the Dry Valley Rodeo. And Matt's got a lot riding on its being a success."

At the rodeo office, two small rooms at the back of the dance hall, a receptionist told the Hardys that Matt was out at the stables. They followed her directions, driving the car down a rutted dirt road behind the arena, until they came to a double row of cinder block stalls. Frank noticed a group of cowboys milling around the last stall.

"Looks like there's something going on up ahead," Joe said.

Frank parked the car. Before either of the Hardys got out, they saw Matt break away from the other cowboys and rush toward them. He tore the passenger door open and reached across Joe for the mobile telephone on the dashboard.

"What's up?" Joe asked, startled.

"No time to explain," he told them, quickly pushing the buttons on the phone. After a short pause, he spoke quickly into the receiver.

"Doc, we've got a very sick animal out here. It looks like someone mixed salt in with the oats. You've got to get here on the double." Matt spat out his orders and hung up the phone.

"That was the veterinarian," Matt explained as Frank and Joe piled out of the car. "Buck Fuller's horse, Rocket, has been poisoned. The poor animal is down on the ground, rolling around in pain. If the vet doesn't get here in time, that horse is going to die!"

Chapter

4

FRANK CROWDED INTO the stall with a dozen cowboys. Joe and Matt were right behind him. Peering over shoulders and hats, he made out a big jet black horse lying on its side in a pile of hay. The animal was panting heavily, and foam coated its muzzle. Its large, liquid eyes were stricken with pain. Buck Fuller was kneeling beside Rocket, gently stroking the horse's head and speaking in soft soothing tones. Despite his loving behavior toward the horse, Frank noticed that Buck was tight-lipped with anger.

"How can salt poison a horse?" Joe asked Matt.

"Horses need *some* salt, like all animals," Matt explained. "But if they get too much, it makes their insides swell up." He gestured to a trough at the side of the stall. "Rocket's oats were filled with salt. Someone must have dumped a ten-pound bag in there."

"Did anyone notice anything or anyone unusual?" Frank asked.

Matt shook his head. "It's pretty quiet around here by two or three in the morning. When Buck got here about six to feed Rocket, he noticed that someone had filled the trough. It could have been anyone. That was just before Rocket collapsed."

Just then a short, gray-haired man wearing crumpled chinos and a white shirt pushed his way through the crowd. He was carrying a black bag. Frank guessed that the man was the veterinarian.

"How could salt get into his ration of oats?" the vet demanded angrily, kneeling beside the stricken animal.

"I don't know," Buck said in a tight voice, backing out of the doctor's way. "But I intend to find out."

The Hardys watched the vet pull a huge needle from his black leather bag. He filled it from a small bottle and injected the medication into Rocket so gently that the horse didn't even flinch.

"That'll fix him up," the vet announced, putting the needle back in his black case.

The horse's reaction was almost immediate. The Hardys watched Rocket lift his head from the floor, shake it as if clearing it, and whinny loudly.

Buck moved back to Rocket's side as the horse struggled to his feet. A cheer went up from the crowd, and Frank and Joe were only too happy to join in.

Joe grabbed Frank's elbow and led him outside where they could speak privately. "That salt didn't fall into Rocket's oats by itself, that's for sure."

"Somebody is trying to sabotage Buck's rodeo appearance," Frank agreed.

"Yeah," said Joe. He thought for a moment. "The only one who we know has a motive is Rodeo Rick."

Frank nodded. "Other people might have grudges against Buck, too, though," he pointed out. "Maybe it's time we started asking a few questions."

"And check out any clues," Joe added.

As the cowboys started to drift away, Frank and Joe noticed a husky man dressed in a clown costume appear at the end of the row of stalls. His face was covered with clown white makeup. He wore a plaid shirt and a pair of overalls many sizes too large. Joe nudged Matt.

"Who's that?" he asked.

Matt smiled. "He's our rodeo clown, but why he's in his costume so early I don't know." He waved the man over.

"Bruce, these are some buddies from out of town, Frank and Joe Hardy."

Without waiting for more introductions, the

clown put out his hand. "I'm Kid Clown, but my real name is Bruce Krieger."

Joe took the clown's hand and yelped, jumping back and colliding with Frank. An electric shock from a buzzer concealed in Kid Clown's hand had caught Joe completely by surprise.

"That was—uh—very funny, Bruce," he said, forcing himself to smile. "I didn't know rodeos had clowns."

"I've been a clown all my life," Krieger said, speaking in a high-pitched silly voice. "Figured I should dress up and get paid to make people laugh instead of doing it for free."

"There's more to it than that," Matt interjected. "In the arena, it's up to the clown to keep the bulls away from the riders after they get off. Most of these cowboys would be flat as pancakes if it weren't for guys like Kid Clown distracting the bulls."

"It's a dangerous life!" Kid Clown said, although not very seriously. "I was just on my way over to the arena where some of the boys are practicing for opening day tomorrow. That's why I have all my duds on."

He turned to Frank and Joe. "Hope to see you around again. Enjoy the rodeo."

Kid Clown headed off as Matt went to the rodeo office. Frank and Joe were deciding what to do when they heard hoofbeats. Terri Garcia was galloping up to them on her white horse.

Her face lit up when she saw Frank. She jumped down from her horse.

"I rode over as soon as I heard about Rocket," she said. "Is he okay?"

Frank nodded. "The vet gave him a shot that brought him around, but apparently it was a pretty close call."

"Want to learn to throw a rope?" she asked.

Frank hesitated. He was flattered by all the attention from Terri, but he had to figure out a way of telling her that he already had a girlfriend back home in Bayport.

"Well, if he doesn't I sure do," Joe responded faster than Frank could answer.

"That's a good idea," Frank said quickly. "You can teach Joe, and he can show me later." He turned to his brother. "Meanwhile, I'll look around to see what I can find."

"Sounds great!" Joe enthused, glancing at Terri.

"Okay." Terri sighed wistfully. "Joe it is."

Leading her horse by the reins, she led Joe to a small corral not far from where all the rodeo competitors' campers and RVs were parked. She tethered her horse to the fence and unclipped a coil of rope from her saddle. Joe helped her lug a bale of hay into the center of the ring.

"That's a bull," Terri said, pointing to the hay.

"Sure." Joe smiled, trying his best to turn on all his available charm. "I can pretend."

Terri held the coil of rope casually in one hand

and took up the end with the loop in the other. She swung it over her head twice and let go. Joe watched the loop sail through the air, pulling the length of rope evenly from the coil. It landed perfectly around the bale of hay.

Joe was impressed. "Looks easy," he said. "But I guess it takes practice."

"A little," Terri said. "Here, you try."

Joe took the rope and positioned himself exactly the way Terri had, the coil in one hand and the loop in the other. He swung the loop in the air and let go. It went up and fell flat at his feet.

Terri laughed. "Maybe a lot of practice."

"You're the teacher," Joe said, blushing and smiling at the same time. He handed her the rope.

Joe watched carefully as Terri showed him how to coil the rope, tie a loop in one end, and then how to position himself before he threw the lasso. He was amazed at how many details he had to remember. It wasn't just a matter of whirling a rope through the air, he realized.

"Timing is important," Terri explained patiently. "You have to know exactly when to let the rope go. And give it a little flick with your wrist," she said, demonstrating. "Like this."

Joe found Terri to be a good teacher, and in less than an hour he was roping the bale on two out of three tries.

Even Terri was impressed. And, Joe thought,

she seemed to be having a pretty good time, even without Frank.

"You're a fast learner," the trick roper told Joe. "How about Frank, is he fast, too?"

Joe shrugged. "Faster than I am at some things, I guess."

Terri's dark eyes sparkled in the bright sun. "But you're faster with the girls," she teased.

Joe brushed his blond hair back from his forehead and smiled. "Well, Frank's got a girlfriend back in Bayport. I don't."

He knew Terri had to be disappointed, but if she was, she quickly hid it.

"Tonight's the opening dance here at the rodeo grounds," Terri said. "Are you and Frank coming?"

"You bet," Joe said excitedly. "Say, I could meet you, say at eight, and we could—"

"Thanks, but I'm busy until then, so I guess I'll meet you and Frank there," Terri replied quickly. "Well, I've got to go now, Joe."

Crestfallen, Joe watched Terri untie her horse from the fence and mount him. "Hey, Joe!" she called back as the horse trotted away. "Tell Frank I hope he likes slow dancing!"

Joe stared after Terri as she rode off. After a long moment he started over to the stables. Frank was there waiting for him.

"So how was your lesson?" Frank asked Joe, noticing how glum he was.

"All I got out of it was a few rope tricks," Joe told his brother.

Frank slapped Joe on the back sympathetically. "Hang in there, brother."

"I'm hanging," Joe protested. "But it's you she's after even after I told her you have a girlfriend. Watch out at the dance tonight. She's in for some slow moves across the floor with you."

"Well, my morning was a little more successful," Frank said, digging in his shirt pocket. He took out a small square of torn paper and handed it to Joe. It was soggy, as if it had been in water. Joe unfolded it carefully. It was triangular and had been ripped from a blue package label. *SA* was visible in yellow block letters.

"It was in the trough that held Rocket's drinking water," Frank explained. "It's all I could find, but I suspect whoever poisoned Rocket didn't plan on leaving it behind. That blue and yellow label is a popular brand of salt."

"Did you test it for fingerprints?" Joe asked.

Frank shook his head. "Saw no reason, but if we come across a bag with a piece ripped out of it that matches this . . ."

"How are we supposed to do that?" Joe asked. "Rummage through everyone's garbage?"

"That's one way," Frank agreed.

Joe handed him back the little scrap of salt package. "You can paw through garbage," he said. "I'll concentrate on Terri Garcia."

* * *

After a huge lunch of smoked ham and home fries Aunt Gertrude and Viola Halloran announced to Frank and Joe that they were going shopping in town. "Would you boys like to come with us?" Mrs. Halloran asked.

Joe patted his stomach and checked with Frank. "I don't know about you, Frank, but I'd like to work off some of this food I've been eating."

"Is there anything around the Double X we can do to help out?" Frank offered.

"Maybe Ernie needs some help," Joe suggested.

"Well, Ernie manages the ranch by himself," Mrs. Halloran told them. "Usually he doesn't like other people getting involved. But you can ask."

"I was out there videotaping all morning and I thought he was perfectly charming," Aunt Gertrude said, hoisting her camcorder.

Joe eyed the camera and put on an expression of mock horror. "No, Aunt Gertrude," he cried, putting his arms up to cover his face. "No more pictures!"

Frank grabbed his brother by the arm and steered him toward the door while Joe kept his face hidden. "It's called videophobia, Aunt Gertrude," Frank cracked, pushing Joe outside.

"You'll be sorry when you're not in any of my travelogue," they heard Aunt Gertrude calling as the door closed behind them.

They found Ernie in the barn, pitching hay with a long-handled hayfork.

"Mrs. Halloran said we might be able to give you a hand this afternoon," Joe said eagerly.

Ernie stopped to study Frank and Joe. For a long moment he said nothing. He narrowed his blue eyes, and a piece of straw moved between his lips as he chewed. Finally he said, "You're the nephews of that friend of Viola's, Gertrude?"

Joe brightened. "That's right."

Ernie turned away from the boys and picked up his hayfork. "She near drove me crazy this morning with that camera of hers."

Joe swallowed and looked at Frank. Ernie didn't seem to be taking to them.

"We'd still like to give you a hand, if there's something we can do," Frank said.

"Reckon you fellas can keep yourselves busy without driving me crazy?"

"Sure!" Frank grinned.

"Anything. Just say the word." Joe nodded.

Ernie pointed to a couple of spades lying against a post in the barn. "Each of you get one of them spades," he instructed. Then he pointed to a stall. "And start shoveling. It's called mucking out."

Ernie hoisted his hayfork in one hand, and strode from the barn, leaving the boys alone. Joe could have sworn he heard the old man chuckle as he left.

"Shoveling manure wasn't what I had in mind by helping out," he said quietly. "I was thinking of mending fences on horseback, building camp-fires. Something a little more glamorous."

The work was hard, and by the end of the afternoon their muscles were sore. Still, Frank pointed out that it was great exercise and took the place of going to the gym for at least one day.

"More like a week," Joe complained, as they headed back to the house to shower.

At eight o'clock that evening, Frank and Joe were ready for the dance. Frank wore white chinos, a blue short-sleeved shirt, and a pair of navy oxfords. Joe was all decked out in his western finest, from his freshly polished boots to his string tie and pearl snaps on his shirt.

Aunt Gertrude and Mrs. Halloran weren't ready when the boys were, and Matt promised to drive them later. Since it was such a balmy night, Frank and Joe decided to walk over to the rodeo grounds. They could hear country music as they strolled up the road to the dance hall.

"The music's by Jason Hughes and the Prairie Dogs," Frank commented as they neared the entrance and the music grew louder. "Matt told me they've already cut a few records."

"They sound real good," Joe said. "Of course, I've always liked country music."

"Yeah, right," Frank said sarcastically. "Ever since you bought those western duds."

Just then the music halted abruptly, right in the middle of a song.

"That's weird," Joe said.

"Come on!" Frank broke into a run and Joe took off after him. They burst through the double front doors into the dance hall. It was like a barn inside, with thick wooden posts and beams dividing the huge dance floor from the tables and chairs that had been set up along the sides. Everyone had cleared the dance floor and was standing in a circle around it.

Frank immediately saw what the problem was. Buck Fuller and Rodeo Rick, only feet apart, were standing facing each other on the dance floor. Loretta was beside Buck, trying to pull him away.

Frank and Joe froze.

"Buck looks pretty angry," Frank muttered. "In fact, they both do," he added, observing that both men had their hands clenched into fists.

"Nobody hurts my horse and gets away with it, Rick!" Buck shouted.

"I wouldn't waste my time on that nag of yours, Buck," Rick shot back. "He's about ready for the glue factory, anyway. And your career is going down the tubes when folks find out you're a jailbird!"

Joe watched Loretta, her eyes wide with fright, tug at Buck's arm. "Please, Buck," she begged. "Don't cause trouble. Let's go back to the—"

"I didn't start this, but I'm not going to run

from it," Buck shouted. He shook Loretta's hand from his arm. "Leave me alone," he snapped.

Loretta turned red with embarrassment and anger. "All right," she said coldly. "Do whatever you want. Just leave me out of it—forever!" The Hardys watched as Buck's wife spun around and rushed past them out the door.

Suddenly they heard a high-pitched voice taunt, "Whack him one, Buck! Don't be chicken!"

Frank and Joe spun around in time to see Kid Clown, still in full clown regalia, push his way to the front of the crowd. "Come on, Buck, sock him!" the clown chanted again.

Frank heard static through the speakers around the dance floor. He saw Jason Hughes, lead singer of the Prairie Dogs, pull the mike off the stand.

"That's right, Buck!" he taunted. "Show us you're a man and slug him!" More shouts came from around the room.

"Let's try to get Buck and Rick apart," Frank said quickly to Joe, "before the whole room blows up and everyone starts fighting."

His brother nodded. Just as the Hardys moved forward, Rick edged up closer to Buck.

"You wouldn't dare," Rodeo Rick snickered, almost nose to nose with Buck now. "You'd get hurt."

"Oh, yeah! We'll see who gets hurt!" With those words, Buck swung his fist in a lightning arc, catching Rick on the jaw.

THE HARDY BOYS CASEFILES

Frank watched Rick stagger back from the force of the blow. He raced forward to place himself between the warring cowboys when suddenly someone pushed him back. In less than a second dozens of cowboys had jumped onto the floor and were taking sides, their fists ready for battle!

Chapter

5

"WE'VE GOT TO STOP this before someone gets seriously hurt!" Frank yelled as bedlam broke out. The dance floor was crowded now with fighting cowboys. In the middle of the melee, Frank saw Buck and Rick slugging it out.

"You grab Rick!" Frank shouted. "I'll take Buck!"

The brothers rushed across the dance floor, dodging blows left and right. When Frank and Joe reached the fighting rodeo stars they noticed a third man—Bruce Krieger, still in his Kid Clown outfit. He was dodging back and forth between the two fighters—egging them on with taunts.

Joe shoved Kid Clown out of the way, yelling, "You better shut up, Krieger, or you'll answer to me!"

Krieger's big painted clown's grin made it seem as if he were enjoying the brawl immensely. He gave Joe an innocent shrug and scampered out of the way.

Joe slammed into Rodeo Rick like a tackle taking out a quarterback. Together, they sprawled on the slippery dance floor. Joe quickly shifted his weight and got Rick into a hammerlock. Frank's tackle took Buck waist-high and bashed them both into the middle of a crowd of angry Rodeo Rick supporters. Frank rolled the startled Buck over and quickly applied a wrestling hold that kept the man under his control.

"This is crazy, Buck!" Frank told the rodeo star. "You can't accuse someone unless you can prove it!"

"All right," Buck agreed, relaxing. "Let me go. I'm done fighting—at least for now."

Across the dance floor, the brawl was scaling down, as the fighters were separated by other men. Joe got up off Rodeo Rick and helped him to his feet. Rick's face was red with anger. He glared at Buck, his eyes filled with hatred.

"Chill out," Joe urged the rodeo star, blocking his path so he couldn't fly at Buck again.

"I'm going to get that guy," Rick snarled in a low, nasty voice. "I'll fix him for good."

Just then Joe heard the country band strike up a lively polka. Jason Hughes, the lead singer, grabbed the microphone. "Y'all calm down and get back to some dancing now," he shouted. "Let's just pretend this little ruckus never happened."

"Sounds good to me," Joe said to Rick.

"Well, it ain't good enough for me," Rick growled back. He pushed past Joe and stomped out of the dance hall.

Joe moved over to where Frank was standing with Buck, near the main entrance to the dance hall. Already couples were moving to the center of the room and starting to dance. Unlike Rick, Joe noticed, Buck had calmed down—and even seemed a little shame-faced about causing the disturbance.

"Guess I really made a mess of things with Loretta," the rodeo star told Frank, patting a welt on the side of the face where Rick had hit him.

"Go and talk to her," Frank suggested.

Buck nodded. "Sure," he said, not very hopefully. "But I think I just blew my last chance with her."

He spun around and strode through the big double doors that led out into the warm night. Just as he left, Frank and Joe saw Matt, Mrs. Halloran, and Aunt Gertrude walk in. Ernie was with them, too, spiffed up in clean jeans and a bright purple cowboy shirt. As usual Aunt Gertrude had her camcorder glued to her eye and slowly panned the room.

"You just missed all the action, Aunt Gertrude!" Joe called out.

Their aunt lowered the camera and glared at her nephew. "We heard what happened," she told him. "And you don't need to sound so gleeful about the fact that I missed taping it. I don't want a silly old cowboy brawl in my travelogue."

Matt walked over to the Hardys. Frank noticed that the young man's face was pale, and worry lines were etched across his forehead. It had to be tough to put a rodeo together—even without escaping bulls, poisoned horses, and fistfights at the opening dance.

"Are you guys all right?" he demanded first.

Frank and Joe nodded.

"I heard about the fight just as we drove in the gates," he told them. "Was anyone hurt?"

Before he could answer, Frank felt an arm wrap itself around his waist.

"Want to dance?" Terri Garcia stood beside him, gazing at him intently with her dark eyes. Just then Jason Hughes and the Prairie Dogs launched into a slow number, and a long, slow ring of whirling couples began to circle the dance floor.

Frank looked for Joe. He knew Joe liked Terri a lot, and the last thing he wanted to do was stand in his brother's way. If Joe was disappointed, Frank couldn't tell. A pretty blond girl had him engrossed in a conversation.

"You guys get out there with the ladies,"

Matt told the brothers. "You've seen a few bad times at the rodeo. Enjoy the good ones."

Frank smiled at Terri. "Sure." A moment later they swung onto the dance floor.

Before the evening was finished, Frank and Joe, Terri and the blond girl, whose name was Joan, had met several other young people and traded dance partners back and forth. Joan and Terri gave Frank and Joe lessons in western line dancing, and the boys even tried some square dancing—with hilarious results. Since they didn't know the calls, they constantly moved in the wrong direction.

For the last dance of the evening, Joe was waltzing with Joan again, and Frank with Terri.

"Look thataway, Frank," Joe drawled, gesturing with his chin to the far side of the floor.

Frank pulled back from Terri. To his surprise, Aunt Gertrude was dancing—with Ernie. The couple was whirling merrily around and around as if they had been dance partners forever.

"They're the perfect couple," Frank said, and laughed.

"At least she put down the video camera for a while," Joe agreed.

Frank and Joe said goodbye to Terri and Joan and left the dance hall with Mrs. Halloran, Aunt Gertrude, and Ernie at midnight. The rodeo was to begin at ten o'clock the next morning.

As Frank and Joe got ready for bed, Frank found his thoughts returning to the events of the last two days and who might be trying to sabotage Buck.

"We'll have to do our best to keep Buck and Rick apart, or we'll have a rerun of the fight tonight," he said to Joe as he crawled into bed.

His brother nodded. "That's the last thing Matt needs. He's under a lot of pressure."

"Maybe we should keep our eyes on Kid Clown," Frank suggested. He threw back his sheet. "The way he was egging Rick and Buck on was kind of weird."

"And what about Jason Hughes," Joe pointed out. "He was telling Buck to slug Rick from the microphone. I wonder why those two were pushing so hard for a fight?"

"I don't know," Frank said, reaching to turn out the light. "But we'll find out."

When Frank opened his eyes the next morning, he saw the day was clear and warm. His first thoughts were about opening day at the rodeo, and he got out of bed in a flash. Once again Viola Halloran had a huge breakfast already waiting for the boys. Matt had left for the rodeo grounds at six to check last-minute details.

By ten o'clock Frank and Joe were sitting in the arena with Aunt Gertrude and Mrs. Halloran, sharing four center front-row seats. Aunt Gertrude snapped a fresh cassette into her camcorder and started to pan the arena.

Joe craned his neck to examine the crowd.

The arena held about five thousand people, he figured, and it didn't look as if there was one empty seat. On one side of the arena the seats were in the open air. On the other side, where they were sitting, a metal roof shielded the spectators from sun and rain. Wherever he looked, he saw row upon row of men and women in cowboy hats.

"That's where the judges must be," Frank said to Joe, pointing to a glass box built above the bleachers at the far end of the arena. The giant Dry Valley Rodeo sign was above that.

Just as he spoke, "The Star Spangled Banner" burst from speakers around the arena. When the anthem ended, Joe hadn't even sat when Terri Garcia burst out of a chute at the end of the arena, riding her white horse at a full gallop. Around him, Joe heard nothing but a deafening roar as the audience cheered the trick roper. He watched Terri swing her lasso, the rope going so fast it was no more than a blur over her head.

Intrigued, Joe watched her spin a gigantic loop and flash it out in front of her horse. It hovered there, circling around and around.

"It's like she's defying gravity!" Joe exclaimed, not taking his eyes from Terri for a moment. Next he saw Terri urge her horse forward. The horse ran through the loop. Then Terri reversed the rope and pulled the loop forward, as her horse stepped through by backing up.

The audience cheered and applauded, and Joe

found himself whistling as loudly as anyone. Terri waved to the crowd, still spinning her lasso, making figure eights and long ovals out of the rope as she rode around the perimeter of the arena.

Terri rode two circuits of the arena without repeating a single trick. Then Joe watched her gallop back into the chute and out of sight.

Joe was on his feet, cheering wildly. Frank stood up, too, clapping hard. The people around them got up, until soon the entire audience was giving Terri a standing ovation.

When the applause finally began to die down, a voice came over the public address system. Frank and Joe sat back down and listened as the announcer, with a friendly, down-home Texas drawl, welcomed them to the Dry Valley Rodeo.

"What's first?" Joe asked, flipping through his program.

"Bull riding," Frank told him. "And guess who the first rider is? Rodeo Rick."

They listened as the announcer explained that there were two judges for the event, and that each judge could award up to twenty-five points for the rider, and another twenty-five for the animal, depending on how hard it bucked. A perfect score was one hundred, after both judges had added their points together.

"Each rider has to remain on the bull for eight seconds to complete a ride," the announcer finished.

"Cool," Joe exclaimed. "Points for the animals, too."

An expectant silence fell over the arena. Frank and Joe leaned forward as the gate of chute number one swung open, and a great black bull burst through. It was hurling its twelve hundred pounds of solid muscle in all directions. On its back, Rodeo Rick sat, tall and strong, his free hand moving in the air with the rhythm of the bull.

"Now I know what Matt meant when he said the mechanical bull was half as mean as the real ride!" Joe told Frank.

He watched the bull spin, throwing a thick cloud of dust and grit in the air as it thundered across the dirt arena. The great beast hurled the rear half of its body upward, then from one side to the other, trying to slingshot Rodeo Rick off its back.

"Look at him hang on!" Frank cried, scarcely able to believe how a man could do it. He heard the eight-second buzzer. Rick jumped from the bull's back and hit the ground running. Frank saw him race toward a nearby gate that rodeo helpers were holding open for him. The bull wasn't far behind.

"There's Kid Clown!" Joe shouted, pointing across the arena. The rodeo clown had jumped over one of the chutes into the ring and was racing toward the bull, waving his arms. The angry bull bolted in his direction.

"Go for it!" Joe shouted as the clown ran toward an open chute. When he was almost there, Kid Clown spun around to face the bull, flapping his arms like a bird trying to take off. All around the Hardys, the audience burst into laughter. Just when the bull had almost reached him, Kid Clown hopped up and over a metal gate. The bull kept charging—right into the open chute. Two cowboys swung the gate shut behind the angry animal.

"Wow!" Frank exclaimed. "That takes a lot of guts."

"You're not kidding." Joe nodded, with new admiration for Bruce Krieger. "I bet rodeo clowns have short lives if that's what they do for a living."

"Wait." Frank put up his hand. "The judges are announcing the score."

Again a hushed silence filled the arena. When the announcer read out a score of 90 for Rodeo Rick's ride, the crowd went wild.

"Any second now it will be Cowboy Buck's turn," Aunt Gertrude announced after the cheering had died down. She turned her camcorder to the arena. "I want to catch every second of his ri—"

Before Aunt Gertrude finished her sentence, Joe saw Buck explode out of the second chute, riding a mean-looking bull. Aunt Gertrude started videotaping as Joe gripped the steel railing in front of his seat. He leaned forward to watch the death-defying ride.

The bull launched itself at the cloudless sky, swinging its hind quarters four feet into the air. Joe watched Buck hang on as if he were riveted to the bull's back. With his free hand, Buck grabbed his hat from his head and waved it at the people in the stands, even while the bull bucked madly.

"Awesome!" Joe cried. "Now I know why Buck's the best."

Just then Buck shook strangely and his hat fell from his hand. The rodeo rider seemed to go limp before Joe's eyes. Then Buck slumped forward and was tossed to the ground like a broken doll.

"What's happening?" Joe cried, grabbing Frank's shoulder. An eerie sound swept through the arena, like the moan of a strong wind. It was the audience, groaning with concern.

"I don't know but—" Frank stopped when he saw the bull spin around, its horns glinting. It lowered its head to gore the unmoving figure sprawled in the middle of the arena.

Somewhere in the packed audience, Joe heard a woman scream. When he glanced around, he saw all the spectators on their feet, their faces reflecting their horror.

"Come on, Joe!" Frank shouted. "We've got to get that bull away from Buck!"

"I'm right behind you!" Joe cried.

The Hardys swung over the metal railing in front of their seats. When Joe's feet hit the ground, the bull was starting its run to Buck's limp body. He reached down and scooped up a handful of dirt.

"Help Buck!" Joe told Frank. "I'll take care of the bull."

He ran to the center of the arena and hurled the handful of dirt at the bull's head as it passed him. The bull skidded to a halt, waving its head angrily from side to side. Then the animal focused on Joe and lowered its head.

Joe froze, his eyes casting about for the best place to run. Just then Kid Clown raced out a gate under the announcer's booth and into the arena, honking the rubber bulb of a horn he had strapped to his chest. Several other cowboys had jumped into the arena, too, and were running across the dirt, waving their arms and shouting.

Joe watched the bull raise its head and look left and right, as if it were confused. Finally the bull swung around and thundered after the rodeo clown.

Krieger moved faster than Joe thought anyone could in baggy oversize jeans and floppy shoes. He led the raging bull into an open chute, and two cowboys quickly swung the steel gate shut. The clown hopped over a fence to safety.

Frank had reached the center of the arena and was kneeling beside Buck's limp body. The rodeo rider was lying face up, and a crimson stain was spreading slowly across the front of his shirt. Two paramedics with Red Cross armbands ran over to join Frank. They were carrying a stretcher.

"He's unconscious and bleeding," Frank said quickly. "But—"

The paramedic bent over the still figure. As he straightened up, Frank met his eyes.

"That's not a rodeo injury," the paramedic said.

"You're right," said Frank. "It's a gunshot wound!"

Chapter

6

"I CAN'T BELIEVE Buck was shot," Frank told the paramedic as he heard Matt Halloran rushing over to join them.

"I was up in the announcer's booth," Matt said, panting to catch his breath. "How's Buck?"

Frank told him about the shotgun wound as the paramedics eased Buck onto the stretcher and carried him to the waiting ambulance for the trip to the Dry Valley Hospital.

Frank watched Matt as he took in the crowds that filled the bleachers, utter confusion on his face.

"I—I don't know what to do," Matt admitted. "Should I cancel the rodeo?"

"Why ruin everything for all these people who've waited all year for this?" Frank said. "Just have the announcer say Buck was injured but that the rodeo will go on."

Matt nodded, thinking carefully about Frank's advice. "You're right, Frank. The rodeo must go on, but in the meantime, I've got to find out who tried to kill the star of our show."

"We'll help you find out, Matt," Frank offered. "We'd like to look around the rodeo, ask some questions—"

"Thanks!" Matt exclaimed, appearing to be slightly relieved. "You have free rein to look anywhere on the rodeo grounds. I can use all the help I can get right now." He spun around and headed back to the announcer's booth.

Frank and Joe ran out to the ambulance waiting at the rear of the arena. With its lights flashing and its siren howling, the ambulance lumbered away from the arena and onto the road. Frank and Joe watched as three police cars pulled up to the arena at the same time. Uniformed police officers poured from the cars and began to spread out into the arena. A burly man wearing a blue blazer and white cowboy hat left one of the cars and strode up to the Hardys.

"I'm Detective Davis," he said. "You fellows witnesses?"

"Sure, along with about five thousand other people," Joe commented.

"You're not from around here, are you?" Davis asked. He had small, icy blue eyes sunk deep in a large, ruddy face.

"No. We're visiting Matt Halloran and his mom during the rodeo," Frank explained.

"Well, we'll have to take a statement," Davis said. "Now I have others to speak to," he said as he walked away.

As Davis left, Terri Garcia rushed over to Frank. "How is Buck?" she asked, her dark eyes filled with worry. "There's a rumor he was shot!"

"He's alive, but we don't know any more than that," Frank told her.

"I was outside the arena when the commotion started. But when I heard Buck was hurt bad . . ." Her voice trailed off and she looked around. "Where's Loretta. Did she go off in the ambulance?"

"Loretta?" Joe asked. "We haven't seen her." He looked at Frank for confirmation.

Terri seemed surprised. "I know she's around," she insisted. "I saw her outside the arena a few seconds after Buck went down."

Frank noticed Detective Davis not far away, listening to every word. When the detective saw Frank looking at him, he moved closer.

"You mean Buck Fuller's wife, Loretta?" Davis demanded, his narrow eyes searching their faces.

Slowly Terri nodded.

"Looks like we're all thinking the same thing," Detective Davis said. "Everybody in Dry Valley knows Loretta Fuller's the best shot around.

Good enough to pick a cowboy off a bucking bull."

He turned to Terri Garcia again. "Whereabouts did you see Loretta, anyway?"

"Just outside the main entrance to the arena," she said, pointing across the ring to the gate underneath the announcer's box.

"Does she have a dressing room or trailer out here?" Davis asked.

Terri nodded again. "Out in the field where all the RVs are parked."

A uniformed police officer appeared at Davis's side, and the detective turned to him. He held up a plastic evidence bag containing a single shell from a bullet.

"We found this under the bleachers over near the booth," the officer told Davis. "It probably fell from up there," he said, indicating a spot high in the bleachers.

Frank and Joe followed the officer's line of vision. He was pointing to a catwalk high above the booth and just below the big Dry Valley Rodeo sign.

"There's a ladder inside the hollow concrete support for that sign," the officer explained. "And from up there, the sniper would have a clear view of the arena."

Detective Davis nodded. "I think we'd better take a look in Loretta Fuller's trailer to see if there's a gun there that's been fired recently. Round up Judge Rheinhold and get a search permit. He's probably at the barbershop in town, like he usually is this time of day.''

Detective Davis turned back to the Hardys. "One advantage of small-town life, you know where to find people when you need them. You boys tell Matt Halloran I have this whole thing under control.''

Detective Davis sauntered away, leaving Frank and Joe standing alone with Terri. They heard a roar coming from the arena.

"Sounds like the rodeo's started up again,'' Joe observed.

"I have to perform soon,'' Terri told Frank, "but later, after the afternoon events . . .'' She pointed in the direction of the RV park. "My trailer's thataway, cowboy.''

This girl won't let up, Frank thought to himself.

Frank and Joe returned to their seats. Aunt Gertrude and Mrs. Halloran were gone. "Let's drive back to the Double X,'' Frank suggested. "We should probably check on them.'' The rodeo went on all day and the boys knew they could come back later.

"We can also grab a bit of lunch,'' Joe added. He pointed up. "The sun's straight overhead, the time when cowboys eat their noon meal.''

As they approached the red sedan in the parking lot, they could hear the cellular telephone buzz insistently.

Joe picked up the receiver. "Loretta!'' he exclaimed, his eyes meeting Frank's. He listened a moment before answering, "No, Matt's not here. He gave us this car to use." He listened another moment, then put his hand over the mouthpiece and spoke to Frank.

"It's Loretta and she sounds frantic. She's at her father's ranch, a few miles out of town, and she says she needs to see us right away." He added, "She sounds pretty upset."

Frank nodded. "Tell her to stay there. We'll head right out."

Joe repeated Frank's words to Loretta, and hung up. Frank dropped into the driver's seat, and in minutes they were cruising down the highway, back out toward the Dry Valley airport. Following the directions Loretta had given Joe, Frank turned onto a twisting dirt road a few miles farther on.

When they saw a sign that read Flying B Ranch, Tom Baker, Prop., they turned and drove to the wooden gate. Half a mile up that road, a weathered frame ranch house and barn came into view. Frank parked the car next to a battered pickup.

Loretta Fuller rushed from the house and stood on the front porch waiting even before the Hardys were out of their car. Joe could see that Loretta's face was puffy and her eyes red. Tears were still running down her cheeks.

"I gotta get to the hospital to be with Buck," she told Frank and Joe as they reached her.

"But I wanted to talk to you first. I called Matt's car, thinking I'd get him to send you over because I remembered him saying you two are detectives. I don't know what to do."

"Try to calm down, Loretta," Frank said gently. "Then we'll talk."

Loretta swallowed hard and dabbed at her eyes with a balled-up tissue before sitting on a rocker on the porch. "We'll have to talk out here," she said. "My dad's awful sick, and I don't want to disturb him." She gestured around the ranch, shaking her head sadly. "This place is falling apart—just like my marriage to Buck. Dad hasn't been able to work the land and the bank is about to foreclose."

Loretta paused for a moment and took a deep breath before looking from Frank to Joe. She started to cry again. "My biggest worry is that someone is trying to kill Buck."

Joe waited a moment until Loretta had composed herself again. "How did you know Buck had been shot?"

Loretta hesitated. Then she answered, "Jason phoned me. Jason Hughes, the lead singer with the Prairie Dogs. He was there when it happened."

"And you were here all morning?" Frank asked.

"No," Loretta told him. Her brow furrowed. "It was really strange. I got a call from Buck, asking me to meet him this morning outside the arena. I still love him, even though I was mad

68

at him last night. I drove over to the rodeo grounds and waited outside the arena for almost half an hour. Buck never showed up. I—I got angry and left. I came back here.''

"What was going on in the arena when you were waiting outside?" Frank asked.

Loretta closed her eyes, straining to remember. "I heard the national anthem, Rick's ride, and his score. Then the announcer said Buck was going to ride next. I knew he wouldn't be out to meet me then. That's when I got mad and left.''

"When did Jason Hughes call you?" Joe asked.

"Maybe twenty minutes ago," Loretta said. "Just before I called you. I'd just gotten back from the arena when the phone rang here. It was Jason, telling me Buck had been shot.''

Loretta reached out to take Joe's hand, then one of Frank's. "Will you please help Buck? I'm so scared whoever is after him will kill him the next time.''

"We'll do whatever we can to get to the bottom of this," Frank promised.

The sound of sirens wound across the Flying B Ranch. Frank saw Loretta blanch. He turned. Heading up the drive were four police cars, their lights flashing.

"Why—why are they coming here?" Loretta asked. She trembled. "I hope they're not coming to tell me Buck has died.''

"They wouldn't use their sirens for that type

69

of call," Frank assured her. "And it wouldn't take four cruisers, either."

"Then what are they doing?"

"I'm not sure," Joe said, staring at the police cars swinging up to the house. "But we'll find out in a minute."

Clouds of dust billowed in the air when the cruisers pulled to a stop. Detective Davis stepped out of the first one. Joe watched him casually release the flap over his holster, in case he had to draw his revolver.

"Uh-oh," Joe whispered to Frank. "This doesn't look good."

Two officers got out of each of the other cruisers and stood in front of their cars. Most of them rested their hands on the butts of their service revolvers.

Detective Davis walked up the steps to the porch, casting his eyes at Frank and Joe, barely acknowledging them. He turned to Loretta Fuller.

"Loretta, you're going to have to come with us to headquarters. I'd like to ask you some questions in connection with the attempted murder of Buck," he said coldly.

"No!" Loretta shrieked. She backed away from Davis, moving toward Frank and Joe as if for protection. "I love Buck. I wouldn't do anything to hurt him!"

Frank and Joe watched Detective Davis pull a small notebook from his breast pocket and wave it at Loretta. "We've got a signed statement from a witness who places you at the arena when Buck was shot, Loretta. We know what a good shot you are, too."

"But that's ridiculous!" Loretta said, barely holding back her tears. "I'm not the only good shot in Dry Valley!"

"You need more evidence than that to hold someone on suspicion of attempted murder," Frank stated, eyeing Detective Davis.

Davis glared back at him and Joe. "We have more evidence," he said flatly. "You remember that spent shell from a .404 carbine we found in the stands under the announcer's booth? It matches the bullet that went into Buck."

Detective Davis swung back to Loretta. "We obtained a search warrant for your trailer and found a .404 carbine. It smelled of cordite, from the bullet, and the barrel was still warm. We'll have a ballistics report in twenty-four hours. And that's how long I can hold you before charging you with attempted murder."

Chapter
7

DINNER THAT EVENING at the Double X was much quieter that it had been since Frank, Joe, and their aunt Gertrude had arrived in Texas. The day's events at the rodeo were over, and Matt came in late to join them.

Frank watched his new friend play with his food. "I talked to the hospital before leaving the rodeo grounds," Matt told them. "Buck's in a coma. They don't know if he's going to make it."

"With Loretta in jail, poor Buck has no one to turn to, even if he does come through this whole thing," Mrs. Halloran said sadly.

Aunt Gertrude looked across the table at Frank and Joe. "What do you think of Loretta's being arrested? Is she guilty?"

Frank spoke first. "There's some pretty serious circumstantial evidence against her, Aunt Gertrude. A witness placed her near the scene of the crime, and the same make carbine that shot Buck was found in her trailer. Of course, until they finish the ballistics tests on the gun, they won't be sure."

"Frank and I definitely don't see the case as closed yet," Joe said. "We're going to visit Loretta in jail tomorrow and ask her some questions."

Joe turned to Matt, whose plate of food was almost untouched. "Any ideas who might want to kill Buck, Matt?"

Matt shrugged. "At this point, your guess is as good as mine. Buck was popular, but he never had a lot of close friends. He was hot tempered. A lot of people liked him, but they steered clear of him, too."

"Well, my hunch," said Joe, "is that there's more here than meets the eye. I don't think Loretta's the murderer."

"Hunches don't stand up in court," Frank pointed out. "But your hunches have helped us in the past. Maybe you're right this time too. In the meantime, Loretta Fuller is in pretty serious trouble."

The next morning Frank and Joe were up early and at the Dry Valley sheriff's office when it opened at nine. Loretta looked haggard, and

Frank and Joe could tell that she'd been crying most of the night.

After greeting her, Frank asked her a question that had been bugging him. "Why weren't you performing at the rodeo yesterday? You said you had to get ready for opening day when we first met you."

"When I woke up I was feeling a bit out of it and told Matt I couldn't perform. You have to be in perfect shape to do sharpshooting, and I knew I'd blow my performance. It was better to let someone go on for me."

"Tell us more about the phone call from Buck," Joe said to her.

"He just asked me to come to the arena and meet him outside. He said he wanted to apologize for the trouble he'd caused the night before. When he didn't show up, well, it was the last straw as far as I was concerned. That's why I left and drove back to my dad's ranch. I was just so angry."

"How long have you and Buck been married?" Frank asked.

"Two and half years," Loretta said. For a moment a smile lit up her pretty face.

"Do you have any idea who might want to kill him?"

Loretta thought a moment. Slowly she said, "Buck has a bad temper, and he stepped on a few toes on his way to the top. And he's so successful, a lot of top hands like Rick get jealous." She opened her hands in a gesture of helplessness. "I really can't think of anyone specifically, though."

Frank thought a moment. Then he remembered something Buck had said the first time they'd met. "Buck told us he hired a private detective once, Loretta. Do you know what that was all about?"

Loretta nodded. "He was trying to track down a long-lost brother. Buck's parents were killed when he was little, and he has only a few memories of an older brother. The two boys were placed in different foster homes. Since he has no other kinfolk, Buck wanted to track down his missing brother."

"Did the agency find his brother?" Joe asked.

"No." Loretta shook her head. "It was just after we were married, and Buck would have told me if he'd found his brother." She looked from Frank to Joe. "You two will go on searching for whoever did this, won't you? As long as the shooter is out there, Buck's in danger."

"We'll do everything we can," Frank answered firmly.

Joe nodded. "We'd like to look around your trailer and Buck's RV over at the rodeo grounds. Is that all right?"

"Sure," Loretta said, brightening a little. "You have my permission. And I'm still Buck's wife, so you can look in his RV, too. Get the keys from Matt. Everyone who parks a trailer or RV on the rodeo grounds has to leave a duplicate key in the office.''

When Frank and Joe left, they drove straight to the rodeo grounds. Luckily Matt had not gone into the stadium yet and was in his office. After a brief search, he found keys for Loretta's trailer and Buck's RV.

As Frank and Joe made their way to the field where the competitors were camped, they could hear the announcer's voice drifting out over the roar of the crowd.

"I guess what happened to Buck hasn't affected attendance here. At least Matt can be happy about that.''

They found Loretta's trailer at the far end of a row of RVs. The trailer was a tarnished old AirStream that had seen better days.

Joe slid the key into the lock, turned it, and carefully pushed the door open. Inside, the trailer looked even smaller than it had from the outside. Frank and Joe quickly glanced around. One wall had been fitted with brackets to hold rifles and shotguns of various calibers. An open closet door revealed dozens of colorful outfits that Loretta wore for her performances.

Frank noticed three windows—one on each of three sides. The one opposite the door was open a crack. Frank walked over and carefully examined it. Bright scratches had been gouged into the metal frame on both sides.

"Check this out!" he called out to Joe, who moved quickly to his side.

"This window has been pried open, and it was done recently," Frank explained, pointing to the gleaming scratches.

Joe started examining the carpet below the window. He moved his fingers carefully through the pile.

"Look at this, Frank." Joe held up his index finger. On the end of it was a speck of glitter. "Mica. It's all over the carpet right under this window."

Frank joined Joe on his hands and knees, and together they combed through the carpet from one end of the small trailer to the other.

"A trail of mica leads from the window right over to the gun rack," Joe concluded when they were finished. "Are you thinking what I'm thinking?"

Frank nodded. "Someone with mica on their shoes came in that window."

"Right," said Joe. "They stole the rifle, shot Buck, and then put it back real fast to make it look like Loretta did it."

"Maybe," Frank said slowly. "Or maybe Loretta set it up to make it seem like she was framed."

"Do you really think so?" Joe asked.

Frank shrugged. "We have to check out all the possibilities," he pointed out. "We need to find out where mica comes from in Dry Valley.

Someone must have walked on a big pile of it to leave a trail like this."

Frank and Joe finished their search of Loretta's trailer and locked the door carefully. Joe spotted Terri Garcia trotting past on her white horse. The trick roper saw the brothers and rode over.

"Hiya, Frank!" she said enthusiastically, then added with less excitement, "Hi, Joe. Say, I didn't know you guys were detectives."

"Who told you that?" Frank asked.

"I was talking to Matt," Terri said. "He told me you were going to help track down whoever's after Buck. He also said you guys saw Loretta today. How is she?"

"About as good as she can be, given what's happened," Joe told her. "She's scared and upset."

"Do you think she can get a public lawyer?" Terri asked. "I know she doesn't have any money. In fact, since she and Buck separated, every penny Loretta's earned has gone to pay her father's medical bills. The poor man owes money to everybody in Dry Valley. In fact, Loretta told me she'd do—"

Terri stopped midsentence, bringing her hand up to her mouth.

"What were you going to say, Terri?" Joe asked.

"I don't want to make things worse for Loretta," Terri said. "But last week she was telling me how bad off her father was, and that she'd do anything to help him. She even said she was going to try to borrow money from Buck." Terri hesitated, but then added. "If Buck was killed, wouldn't she get all his money?"

"Maybe," Frank said. "That's usually what happens between a husband and wife. But it depends on Buck's will."

"We'll have to check it out," Joe said quietly to Frank. Frank nodded.

"Well, I still don't think Loretta would shoot Buck for money," Terri said. "I have a routine after the bronc riding. See you guys later." She spun her horse around and trotted back toward the arena.

When she was gone, Frank turned to Joe. "Next stop is Buck's RV," he said, pulling out that key. "It's at the other end of the rodeo grounds."

They started walking, and as they passed the arena, Joe heard the announcer introduce Terri Garcia. A wave of cheers and whistles erupted from the audience.

"Looks like I'm not the only one who thinks Terri is beautiful." Joe grinned. "The whistles are louder than the applause."

Just then Frank saw Kid Clown emerge from one of the arena's gates. His face was wet with sweat, and his eye makeup was running down his white cheeks.

"Whew," he panted when he spotted Frank

and Joe. "It was broiling out there. I'm glad Terri's on now." He stopped beside a large, flatbed farm wagon loaded with bales of hay and gently patted his forehead with a bandanna so he wouldn't ruin his makeup. "How's the investigation going, fellows? Have you dug anything up yet?"

Frank and Joe exchanged annoyed looks. It seemed as if everyone knew they were on the case.

"What do you mean by investigation?" Frank demanded.

Even under his clown makeup, Bruce Krieger seemed to be taken aback. "Well, everyone at the rodeo knows you two are a couple of junior detectives," he said. "Word gets around."

"We're still working on the case," Frank said.

"You know what's funny about all this?" Kreiger grinned.

"I don't find anything funny about attempted murder," Joe said.

"Just listen," the clown persisted. "Loretta tried to croak Buck to get his money, but it'll never work. A criminal can't benefit from her crime. So even if Buck dies, his money will go somewhere else. Looks like the laugh is on Loretta." Kid Clown chortled. "I mean, with the law the way it is about criminals not profiting from their crimes, I guess it serves her right. It's too bad his wife's greed had to hurt him."

"No one has proved Loretta did it yet,"

Frank pointed out. "That's for a judge and jury to decide."

"Yeah, right," Kid Clown said doubtfully. "That's why they found that rifle in her trailer."

"I've got a question for you, Bruce," Joe said. "When Buck was shot, why weren't you out in the arena? If it hadn't been for Frank and me jumping into the ring, Buck might have been gored after he collapsed."

Krieger eyed Joe for a moment before answering. Then he said, "As soon as I saw Buck was in trouble I charged out from the chutes. Say, what are you asking me questions for? I'm the guy who saved Buck's life, not the one who tried to take it."

"Nothing personal, Bruce," Joe told him. "I was just wondering."

Bruce glanced at a large, plastic oversize watch on his wrist. "I have to get back to work. See you later, guys." He dashed off, his gigantic overalls flapping as he ran.

"Krieger's awfully interested in who gets what if Buck dies," Frank mused. He and Joe moved away from the hay wagon and continued on to Buck's RV.

"Yeah," Joe agreed, thinking about something. "You know what? I'm not a hundred percent sure, because everything happened so fast yesterday when we jumped into the arena. But I think I remember Kid Clown running into the arena from under the announcer's box, not from the chutes.''

Before Frank could reply, Joe heard the crowd in the stands suddenly burst into wild cheers and yells.

"Somebody must be making a great ride," Joe shouted over the noise.

Frank grinned and was about to say something. He was stopped when he heard the sound of wheels rumbling behind him. He glanced over his shoulder.

"Watch out, Joe!" he shouted.

The hay wagon they'd been standing next to only a few seconds earlier was rolling straight toward them!

Chapter

8

FRANK SLAMMED INTO JOE like a tackle, and the force of the impact carried them both several yards. The brothers lay sprawled on the ground as the hay wagon flew past to crash into the cement wall of the arena. Hay and splinters of broken wood flew all around them.

"What in the world?" Joe sputtered as he slowly picked himself up. He surveyed the broken hay wagon and brushed hay from his jeans. "That was too close. We could have been crushed against that wall like bugs on a windshield."

"Someone must have given that wagon a push," Frank said, getting up and gazing in the direction the wagon had come from. No one was in sight.

"Are you guys okay?" a roustabout called,

running from a gate. "I was up on a catwalk over the bleachers, and I just about screamed my lungs out trying to warn you."

"Did you see the wagon start to roll?" Frank asked. "Was there anyone near it?"

The cowhand shook his head. "No, it was already rolling when I noticed it. I didn't see anyone around except you guys." He studied the wrecked wagon. "Well, I'm sure glad you guys weren't hurt. I better go find someone to get this mess cleaned up."

"Let's check out the spot where the wagon was parked," Frank suggested to Joe.

They retraced their footsteps until they saw ruts from the wagon's big wheels cut into the ground. Two wooden blocks lay off to the side. Frank pointed at them.

"Those were under the wheels to stop it from rolling. Someone must have kicked them out."

"Someone who doesn't want us investigating Buck's shooting," Joe speculated.

Frank nodded. "We should have warned Matt not to tell people we were working on this case. It's too late now since everyone seems to know. We'll just have to be extra careful from now on."

"Let's keep this little incident to ourselves," Joe suggested. "The last thing Matt needs is to start worrying about us, too."

Frank agreed. They continued on to Buck's RV, a gleaming new camper parked next to

Rocket's horse trailer. The Hardys stepped inside and gazed in shock at the interior.

"Someone beat us to it," Frank said. The RV had been ransacked. Drawers and cupboards were opened, the foam mattresses on the beds and couches were overturned, and papers were strewn everywhere.

"We'd better let Detective Davis know about this," Joe pointed out. He felt something stick to his shoe just then and lowered his head to check it out. He'd stepped on the gummy flap of a large manila envelope that was lying on the floor. He bent down and retrieved it, holding it by one corner. A sheaf of papers fell out and landed on a small table. Yellowed newspaper clippings and handwritten letters lay on the table. Frank moved over to stand beside Joe.

"Look at this," Joe said, pointing to one of the articles. "This clipping tells of a car crash that killed a man and woman." He scanned the tiny print of the article below the picture. "They left two small sons behind. This must be about the accident that killed Buck's parents."

Frank pointed to a handwritten letter with Buck's signature at the bottom. "Here's a copy of a letter Buck wrote to the state of Texas, trying to find out where his brother had been placed for adoption."

"Yeah, and look at this one," Joe said. "Buck hired an investigator to try to find out where his brother ended up."

Frank took the letter Joe was pointing to. Stapled behind it was another letter. Frank flipped the first letter over so he could read the second one.

"It's an answer from the detective agency," Frank said, examining a carefully typed letter from a Dallas agency. It was signed by a private eye named Don Hooper. "It's dated a year ago and says they're still looking. And there's an old bill attached for over three thousand dollars."

Joe whistled. "That's a lot of money. I wonder if they found his brother."

"There's nothing here to indicate they did," said Frank. "And remember, Loretta was pretty sure the search had been a failure."

"Let's call the detective agency," Joe said.

"Good idea," Frank agreed. He picked up a cellular telephone on the wall and pushed in the phone number of the agency. He asked for Don Hooper, then listened intently. After a few moments he said thank you and hung up.

"What's up?" Joe asked.

"Don Hooper was killed in a car accident a year ago. Some of his files were burned up in the crash. Buck's was one of them."

A stunned silence fell between the brothers. Joe was the first to speak.

"A dead end," he said quietly.

"Looks like it," Frank agreed. "At least for the moment." He wandered around the ransacked room and found a photograph lying on the floor.

"Hey, Joe, look at this." Joe gazed at it over his brother's shoulder. "It was taken about four years ago, according to the date on the bottom."

Two men were standing side by side, beaming happily with their arms around each other's shoulders. One held a guitar. "That's Jason Hughes!" Joe exclaimed. "The lead singer of the Prairie Dogs. The other one is Buck!"

"Right," said Frank. "And look where the picture was taken." He pointed to a sign that was visible behind the two men. It read Central Texas Prison Farm and Rehabilitation Center.

"That's where Buck said he learned how to do rodeo tricks," Joe said. "Do you think Jason Hughes was an inmate, too?"

"I don't know," Frank answered. "But I'd like to ask Jason Hughes a few questions." He set the photograph down on the table. "Let's get out of here. We'd better tell Matt to call Detective Davis about whoever ransacked this RV."

"Yeah, someone was looking real hard for something in here. I wonder if he found it," Joe said.

Frank nodded slowly. "Or she," he added.

The boys walked back toward the arena. The applause and cheers of the crowd in the seats were muffled but grew louder as they approached. As they passed the back of the arena where the rodeo riders entered, Joe scanned the pens of animals. Calves, broncos, and snorting bulls were all kept in separate corrals, fenced in by steel gates. The pens were separated by narrow chutes through which the cowboys led the animals into the arena.

"Frank," Joe said quietly. "Check out the pen with the bulls. I'm almost positive I saw somebody watching us. Whoever it was pulled his head back real fast when I looked his way."

Frank broke into a loud laugh and tossed his arm casually over Joe's shoulders. "That's a good one!" he said loudly, laughing again. The laughter, though, was phony. Frank had carefully positioned himself to face his brother, but his eyes were focused past Joe to the pens beyond.

"See anything?" Joe whispered.

Frank dropped his arm. "I caught the flash of a shirt," he said quickly. "Someone's in the chute that runs down the middle of the bull pen."

"You ready to do some running?" Joe asked. "Let's grab this guy before he gets away."

Frank nodded. "But let's keep walking to let him get farther into that chute. Then I'll take the front and you take the back, and we'll trap him between us."

"Excellent idea," Joe agreed.

The Hardys started walking again, drawing closer and closer to the bull pen.

"Let's run on the count of three," Frank instructed.

Joe drew a deep breath, and he psyched himself for a dash to the pen. He heard Frank count quietly. When he heard "three" Joe spun around and sprinted for the chute. His feet dug into the sun-baked soil as he raced down the length of the pen.

Frank swung over the high metal fence and into the chute at the other end. "You! Stop!" he shouted, seeing a man in a red shirt race down the chute in the opposite direction. Frank picked up speed, and his quarry ran faster, too. The chute twisted almost ninety degrees. The escaping man shot around the corner and was hidden by the bulls on the other side of the chute.

At the far end of the pen, Joe jumped into the chute and was racing forward just as the man he was pursuing came around the corner where the chute turned. They slammed into each other full force, Joe flying back into the dirt, gasping for breath. When he looked, he saw the man halfway over the fence, climbing into a pen holding a dangerous bull.

"Don't!" Joe yelled.

It was too late. The man vaulted over the fence into the pen.

Frank raced around the corner of the chute just then to see Joe on the ground. "Are you okay?" he asked.

"Yeah," Joe said, getting to his feet. "Come on! He went over the fence and into the pen!"

Frank and Joe climbed the chute and sat balanced on the pen's metal fence. Halfway across the wide pen, a man stood stock still, his back to the Hardys, obviously paralyzed with fear.

Joe watched as a giant black bull put its head down and scratched angrily at the dirt with its front hoof.

"That dude's in big trouble," Joe said urgently. "That bull's going to charge!"

Chapter

9

"DON'T MOVE!" Frank shouted to the man. "We'll try to distract the bull. As soon as he looks away from you, run and get out of the pen. You got that?"

"Yes!"

The man's voice was trembling, but Frank and Joe recognized it immediately.

"That's Jason Hughes!" Joe cried.

"All we have to do now is keep him in one piece," Frank said. "Then maybe we can get some answers out of him."

Frank picked up a clod of dirt and motioned Joe to do the same. They approached the bull carefully, their arms cocked to throw.

"Go for it!" Frank uttered.

Simultaneously, the Hardys threw clumps of

dirt. The bull snorted and spun to trample its attackers. The second the bull moved, Jason Hughes took off for the side of the pen. Joe and Frank waited a moment and then raced across the pen to where Hughes had just jumped over. Together they vaulted the fence.

Jason Hughes, struggling to catch his breath, barely managed to gasp, "Thanks, guys." He was a tall, thin man with stringy brown hair.

"We don't want your thanks," Joe said angrily. "We want to know why you're shadowing us."

"I—I—" Jason stuttered. He took a deep breath. "You guys saved my life," he said. "That bull was going to wreck me. I'll tell you what you want to know. I owe you that much."

He paused and gazed at Frank and Joe, as if he didn't know where to begin. Finally he said, "Buck and I go back a long way."

"Yeah, all the way back to the Central Texas Prison Farm," Joe growled.

Jason Hughes whitened. "How—how'd you guys find that out?"

"Never mind that," Frank snapped. "We're still waiting to hear why you were following us."

Jason Hughes took another deep breath. "I got involved with the wrong people when I was a kid, and I got sent to the pen for burglary. I'd been there for a year when Buck was sent up. I showed him how to get by. While he was learning about rodeo on the prison farm, I was practicing the guitar and writing songs. We were good friends.''

"If you're such good friends, why didn't you do anything to stop that brawl at the dance the other night?'' Frank demanded.

Jason Hughes hung his head, as if he was ashamed. "You're right. I was kind of a jerk that night. Buck and I had a bit of a falling out.''

"What over?'' Frank asked.

"He was working with kids' charities and he wanted to keep his prison record secret. So when Matt Halloran hired my band to play the rodeo here, he told me he was going to pretend he didn't know me.''

"So you're enemies now?'' Joe said.

Jason shook his head quickly. "No, at least, I don't like to think of it that way. In prison Buck and I were really tight, and we got each other through the bad times. Someone's out to get him now, and I heard that Matt's asked you guys to find out who it is. That's why I was following you. I wanted to know what you were up to, what you found out, that's all.''

"Is there anything else we should know about?'' Joe asked.

Jason Hughes hesitated, glancing quickly from Frank to Joe. Finally he nodded. "Yeah, there is,'' he said. "There's someone you guys should be talking to if you want to solve this crime.''

"And who's that?'' Frank demanded.

"Rodeo Rick,'' Hughes answered, staring at

Frank steadily. "I saw him over at Rocket's stall when Buck's horse was poisoned."

"You're a witness!" Frank exclaimed, stunned by Jason Hughes's disclosure. "Why didn't you come forward before?"

Hughes put his hand up as if to fend off blows. "Look, my band's working this rodeo and I don't want to cause trouble by telling tales on major rodeo stars. Besides." He faltered. "All I'm saying is that I saw Rick over at those stables about four-thirty A.M., and he was carrying something under his arm that could have been a bag of salt."

"What were you doing walking around at that time?" Joe demanded.

"Me and the band had been practicing all night. I was walking back to my RV from the dance hall."

"So let's say Rick did poison Rocket," Frank said. "What's he got against Buck?"

Jason gave a rueful laugh. "Everyone on the circuit knows Rick would love to see Buck dead. Ask anyone. Didn't Rick lead a bunch of contestants over to Matt's house to complain about Buck's being an ex-con?"

"We were there," Frank confirmed. "Look, Jason, if you really want to help us find out who wants Buck dead, you can come to us with anything you might hear. Okay?"

Hughes nodded. "Sure," he said. "And thanks.

Buck and I were like brothers once. If I learn anything, you'll hear about it.''

He quickly shook hands with each of the Hardys and left.

"This case is becoming more and more complicated," Joe said.

"It sure is," Frank answered. "At least we know what we have to do now."

"Pay a visit to Rodeo Rick."

Frank and Joe returned to the field with the RVs and trailers and asked where they could find Rick's trailer. Soon they were standing outside an enormous RV, much longer than Buck's, although not nearly so new.

"Bet this baby gets about two miles to the gallon," Joe mused, checking it out.

"There doesn't seem to be anyone around," Frank said, after knocking. The windows of the RV were closed, and there was no answer.

Joe stepped forward and pushed on the door. It swung in. He looked at Frank. "I suggest we wait inside."

Frank went first, up two steps to the driver's seat and then into the cabin. There was a small kitchenette on one side, and then long, cushioned seats running under the windows. Farther back, a partly open door revealed a bedroom. Posters of Rodeo Rick seemed to cover every available space on the walls.

"Rick looks like he's about twenty years old

95

in this poster," Joe said, pointing to a big picture of the rodeo star on a horse, hanging on the wall over a table. "And he must be pushing forty now. He's been at this a long time."

"Look at this one," Frank said. "It must be from fifteen years ago. Seems like he's living in the past, at least when he's in his trailer."

Joe gestured to the counter in the tiny kitchenette. It was covered with empty whiskey bottles. "And drowning his sorrows, too." Then Joe saw a blue package on a shelf in an open cupboard below the sink. He reached down and pulled it out.

"What have we here?" he crowed, holding it up for Frank to see. It was a twenty-pound bag of salt—almost empty. "And look at this. It's ripped." Joe smoothed out the heavy paper bag. He pointed to a place where a triangular bit of the label had been torn off.

Frank pulled out his wallet and opened up one of the inner compartments to remove the folded scrap he'd found in Rocket's water trough. He held it against the label on the salt bag. It fit perfectly.

"At least now we know who salted Rocket's oats," Frank said sadly. Suddenly he heard the door of the RV slam open so hard the glass in the small window almost broke.

"Stand right where you are and get your hands up or I'll blow your brains out!"

Chapter

10

RODEO RICK, a cruel grin on his face, walked into the RV holding a revolver in his right hand. Frank watched him wave the gun back and forth, from him to Joe.

"Just what do you two think you're doing in my trailer?" Rick snarled. "Trying to plant something here that'll tie me in to what happened to Buck?"

"We don't have to plant anything," Joe said bravely. He held up the salt bag for Rodeo Rick to see. At the same time he caught Frank's eye and nodded his head the slightest bit.

"Yeah, Rick, we've got you cold!" Frank shouted.

When Rick instinctively turned his head toward Frank, Joe tossed the salt into the rodeo star's face. Then he brought him down with a crushing tackle that threw Rick across the RV to land against a wall. The revolver flew from his hand and landed on the floor near Frank.

Frank grabbed the weapon and inspected the barrel. "It's empty!" he said.

"It scared you two plenty when I came in here," Rodeo Rick said sullenly. He sat up, rubbing the back of his head. "This is private property—even to friends of the owners who are playing detective."

"Maybe it's time you found out we're not playing," Frank said coolly, watching Rick stand up and ease himself onto a couch.

Joe picked up the bag of salt from the floor. "Maybe you ought to tell us what this is doing here."

A stricken look crossed Rodeo Rick's face. "I like salt," he said tightly. "That's no crime, is it?"

"No," Frank agreed. "But shooting Buck Fuller is." He showed Rick the torn scrap from the salt bag. "This came from Rocket's trough and it matches a tear in that bag. We can prove you tried to poison Buck's horse, Rick. And we also have a witness. So it's about time you came clean and told us the truth."

Frank saw the desperation cross Rodeo Rick's face. "I didn't shoot Buck," Rick assured the Hardys. "I just wanted to scare him enough so that he'd quit the rodeo. I wouldn't kill anybody, not even him. I'm telling the truth." He slumped on the couch, defeated.

"All right, I admit it," Rick said finally. "I salted Rocket's oats."

"And how about letting the bull free when Buck and Matt were out in the middle of the arena with Frank and me," Joe said. "I bet that was your doing, too."

Rodeo Rick lowered his head. "Yeah, I did that, but I didn't want anybody to get hurt, really." He turned from Frank and Joe. "You have to believe me."

"And then you tried to cut us down with that hay wagon today, didn't you?" Joe demanded.

A puzzled look appeared on Rick's face. "Hay wagon? I don't know anything about any hay wagon. What are you talking about?"

Neither Frank nor Joe spoke. They knew enough about questioning a suspect to realize that silence was, at times, more effective than any question.

Rodeo Rick brought his hands up to his face. His voice cracked with emotion when he spoke.

"I didn't have anything to do with no wagon, and I didn't shoot Buck Fuller," he cried. "All I wanted was a couple more seasons of being top hand. I worked hard to get where I am and I don't want some ex-con stealing everything I've worked for."

Frank sighed. "Do you have an alibi for the time Buck was shot?"

Rick raised his head. "Sure I do," he said eagerly. "I'd just finished my ride. I was back at the gates, talking with the boys. Hank and Boone, they'll tell you I was there. You go ask!"

"We will," Frank said firmly. "And I'm going to have to tell Matt about the other things you've been up to, Rick. What happens after that is up to him."

"I feel kind of sorry for Rick," Joe said as they searched for Matt Halloran. "He's put his whole life into the rodeo and for years he was a big winner. It really bothers him that Buck's taking over as the top bull rider."

"There aren't that many rodeo stars pushing forty, so that's an accomplishment in itself," Frank responded. "And Rick should know you can't stay on top forever. He didn't have the right to hurt Rocket, though, or to let that bull out."

"You've got that right," Joe said. "You think he's telling the truth about not shooting Buck?"

Frank shrugged. "At least he gave us an alibi that should be easy to check out."

The Hardys made their way over to the rodeo office behind the dance hall, stopping for a quick lunch of hot dogs and sodas. When they finally arrived at the office, Matt was out, but the secretary told them to wait in Matt's office and make themselves comfortable.

Joe dropped into a long, plush sofa that took

up one end of the office. He looked around at the framed photographs that lined the walls, each one portraying a high point in a rodeo.

"Loretta and Rodeo Rick are still our best suspects," Frank said, sitting in an armchair near Matt's cluttered desk. "Loretta's upset about her marriage going sour and she needs money to help her father. Rodeo Rick is jealous of Buck and stands to lose lots of prize money if Buck keeps outriding him."

"My gut feeling is that neither of them did it," Joe said finally. "I think Loretta still loves Buck, even though they're having problems. And Rick—well, he seemed pretty sure of his alibi. It should be easy enough to check."

"So if they didn't do it, who does that leave?" Frank asked.

"Me and you," Joe joked. "And I'm sure I didn't do it. What about you?"

"I have an alibi." Frank laughed. "I was with you, remember? Is that good enough to keep me from being—" Frank saw an expression of astonishment spread across Joe's face as he was talking. "What's the matter?" he asked.

Joe pointed to a pair of leather boots resting on a mat near the office door. They were encrusted with dried mud, and the sun shone through a window directly on them. The bright light picked out bits of glittering mica. Joe got up and picked up one of the boots, examining it closely. He handed it to Frank.

"It's just like the mica we found in the carpet at Loretta's."

Joe stopped when Matt walked in the door of the office. He greeted the Hardys with a boisterous smile. "Running a rodeo is harder than it looks," he said. "There are a million details I have to stay on top of. I'm glad the crowds haven't dropped off much since Buck was shot, though."

"We've been asking questions," Joe told Matt, "and thought we should bring you up to date on a few things."

Matt stared flatly at Joe. "You mean about Buck?" He shook his head. "Looks like the police have the case solved. The ballistics tests came back today and proved that the bullet that hit Buck was fired by the rifle they found in Loretta's trailer. Detective Davis formally charged her with murder, and the judge is asking for fifty thousand dollars' bail."

Joe whistled quietly, casting a quick look at Frank. His brother was as shocked as he was. "That's a lot of money," he said.

"Sure is," Matt agreed. He moved behind his desk and sat down. "Until Loretta can raise it—which isn't likely—she'll stay in jail."

Frank shook his head unhappily. "Joe and I think there's more to this than that, Matt. First of all, someone sent a hay wagon in our direction this morning, hoping it would crush us."

Matt looked shocked. "That was you! One of

my hands told me about that accident, but I didn't realize—"

"Loretta was in jail when that happened," Joe pointed out.

"That's not all," Frank added. "Buck's trailer was ransacked by someone. And Rodeo Rick had some things to say to us, too." Quickly he explained what had happened in Rick's RV.

Matt shook his head sadly. "A lot of people have been saying Rick's washed up, but I didn't realize how desperate he was."

"By the way," Frank said, holding up the boot in his hand. "Are these yours?"

"Yeah, my climbing boots. Why? You want to borrow them?"

Frank shook his head. "No, I was just wondering where you'd been that you got bits of mica on them."

Matt laughed. "I do all my climbing over at Sparkle Bluff. It's about an hour out of Dry Valley, a tall cliff face with layers of mica in the rock. The rangers have hammered in pitons for rappelling down the whole face of the rock. We should go out there after the rodeo."

"Rappelling?" Joe asked. "Pitons? I haven't done much mountain climbing."

"Pitons are steel stakes that are driven into the stone to support a person's weight," Matt explained. "Rappelling is done by hooking a rope into the pitons and hopping down the cliff.

A good rappeller can get down hundreds of feet of sheer rock face in a matter of seconds.''

"Wow!'' Joe exclaimed. "I'd like to try it sometime. When did you last go?''

"About three weeks ago,'' Matt said quickly, glancing at his watch. "Say, I have to get back up to the judge's booth before the next event. I'll see you guys at dinner.'' Matt took off.

Frank turned to Joe when he was gone. "One of two things just happened.''

Joe's expression was puzzled. "What's that?''

"Either the police have cracked the case and the guilty party—Loretta—is behind bars. Or we add Matt to our list of suspects.''

"Matt?'' Joe cried. "You're kidding!''

"Not until we find another explanation for that trail of mica in Loretta's trailer,'' Frank concluded.

That evening the group around the big dining room table at the Double X Ranch was somber.

"I called the hospital,'' Mrs. Halloran said. "They told me Buck is still in a coma.''

"How long do they think the coma will last?'' Matt asked his mother.

Mrs. Halloran shook her head sadly. "Some comas have been known to last for years.'' Her voice trembled as she added, "They told me not to get my hopes up too high for poor Buck.''

"Such a terrible thing,'' Aunt Gertrude said sadly across the table to her nephews. "I feel so awful for that poor Loretta, being stuck in a cell when her husband may be dying. Do you still suspect her in the shooting?''

"I'm afraid so," Frank answered.

Aunt Gertrude helped herself to a slice of roast beef from a plate that Matt passed her. "I haven't wanted to watch my videotape," she said. "I was taping the whole thing when Buck was shot. My finger kind of froze on the button of my camcorder."

Frank and Joe both pushed their chairs back at the same time, their suppers suddenly forgotten. "Aunt Gertrude," Joe said, "we need to see that tape right now. And I promise," he added quickly, "I'll never tease you about your travelogue again."

"Well, all right," Aunt Gertrude said. "But I won't watch it. Seeing that sight once was enough for me."

Frank and Joe excused themselves from the rest of the meal and took their aunt's camcorder into the Hallorans' den. Joe hooked up the cables from the camera to the television set and started the tape rolling. He fast-forwarded to the opening scenes of the rodeo, and finally found the section where Buck burst out of the chute, riding the bull.

"Here it comes," Joe said tensely.

Frank's eyes were glued to the television screen. He watched the rodeo star ride the bull and casually take off his hat with his free hand.

Then he watched as Buck's grin left his face. The man crumpled and fell from the bull's back onto the dirt of the arena. A moment later Frank watched as he and Joe raced across the arena, waving and shouting to distract the bull.

"There we are," Frank said.

"Yeah," said Joe. "And there's Kid Clown coming in from the left to keep the bull away from Buck. And there's a paramedic jumping the—hold it, Frank!" Joe cried. He bent over the camcorder and rewound part of the tape.

Once again Frank and Joe watched Buck fall from the bull and Bruce Krieger dash in from the left, his huge overalls flapping as he ran.

"That's it!" Joe cried. "Now I know for sure. Look where Krieger comes into the arena—from near the announcer's booth!"

"Well, yeah, I see that," Frank said. "But what about it? Sure, he was a few seconds late, but he got out there in time to distract the bull, didn't he?"

"Yes, he did," Joe agreed. "But he told us he came in from the chutes."

"He did," said Frank. "But I don't understand, Joe. If you're thinking of Kid Clown as a suspect, he's got an alibi right here on tape. And five thousand people—including us—saw him in the arena when Buck was shot."

"Not really," Joe objected. "Sure he's on tape, and sure he was in the arena. But not until *after* Buck was shot and fell off the bull!"

Chapter

11

"I COULDN'T SLEEP last night, thinking about what we saw on Aunt Gertrude's video," Joe said to Frank as they were walking down the stairs at the Halloran home the next morning. The sun had barely cleared the eastern horizon.

"I still think this is a long shot," Frank commented. "Kid Clown may just have forgotten where he came into the arena."

"But his version conveniently puts him at the side of the arena far from where the shot was fired. According to the videotape, he came from a gate that was right under the catwalk where the sniper who shot Buck was hiding."

Frank nodded reluctantly. "Yeah, but there's no way he could get from the catwalk down to the arena so fast. And besides, what's his motive? You have to prove motive, too.''

Joe sighed. ''Maybe by the end of the day we'll have some answers to these questions.''

When they walked into the kitchen Matt Halloran was already there, drinking a glass of juice.

''We're ready,'' Joe said immediately.

Matt threw the Hardys a couple of apples from a bowl on top of the fridge. ''There's no need to starve while you're busy being detectives.'' He laughed. ''I guess I can't persuade you to just drop the investigation and enjoy the rodeo. The police seem to think the case is closed.''

''All the police have closed is a jail door—on Loretta Fuller,'' Joe insisted. ''We need another day to look around and check some things out.''

''Like Rodeo Rick's alibi,'' Frank said. ''He said those two cowboys, Hank and Boone, were with him.''

Matt nodded. ''I know those men, and they're honest Dry Valley old-timers. If Rodeo Rick was with them, they'll tell you truthfully. I still haven't decided what to do about Rick. I should call the police and let them decide. . . .''

''There's one other thing you can help us with,'' said Joe, interrupting his trailing thought. ''Loretta says Buck phoned her the morning he was shot and asked her to meet him at the rodeo. The phone company should have a computer record of the number that the call to Loretta was made from."

Matt seemed puzzled. "What use is that information?"

"What if it wasn't Buck who called her?" Joe said. "What if someone else did, disguising his voice to sound like Buck. He could have lured Loretta to the rodeo to frame her—after stealing the rifle from her trailer?"

Frank slapped his brother on the back. "I think your theory's a long shot, but you've really thought it through, haven't you?"

Joe smiled sheepishly. "Most of the night," he said.

"So what do you want me to do?" Matt asked.

"You know anyone at the phone company who can look at those records?"

Matt thought a moment. "I'll make some calls and see what I can find out," he said.

Matt drove the Hardys over to the rodeo in the red sedan, then turned the car over to them.

"I left my four-wheeler over by the office last night and hitched a ride with a friend," he said. "I won't be needing this car for the rest of the day."

"How will we find Hank and Boone to ask them about Rick's alibi?" Frank asked.

Matt glanced at his watch. "Give me half an hour and I'll have them in my office," he said.

"Great!" said Joe. "In the meantime Frank

and I want to check out the scene of the crime again."

"In the arena?" Matt asked.

Frank nodded. "Before the crowds arrive."

The Hardys and Matt separated, with Frank and Joe walking through the gate under the announcer's box into the arena. Two hours before the day's events began, it was completely deserted. The tiers of seats climbed high in the early morning sun. The sounds of horses, calves, and bulls moving around in their pens at the far end were the only things to disturb the silence.

Joe trotted over to the spot just below one side of the announcer's booth. "Here's where the police found the bullet shell," he said.

Frank joined his brother. They both looked high above them at the steel catwalk over the announcer's booth. On the side facing away from the arena, the giant sign, lit at night by hundreds of lightbulbs, spelled out Dry Valley Rodeo Grounds.

"I guess the catwalk's used to change burned-out bulbs," Joe said.

Frank pointed straight ahead, to where a gate opened into the arena. "According to the videotape, that's where Krieger ran into the arena. But there's no way he could have gotten from the catwalk down there in anything less than five minutes. On the tape, he was in the arena less than a minute after Buck was shot."

Joe nodded slowly, gazing from the catwalk

down to the arena, squinting against the bright Texas sun. "You're right," he admitted. "I guess it was a long shot."

Sensing Joe's disappointment, Frank made a suggestion. "Let's backtrack Krieger's steps."

Together the Hardys took the gate the rodeo clown had used. It led to a tunnel under the bleachers. A moment later Frank and Joe found themselves in front of a hollow support for the bleachers and the announcer's box. It was made of poured concrete, and an unlocked metal door was set in the wall.

"It must lead right up to the catwalk," Frank observed, raising his head. He opened the metal door. The interior of the support was about a yard in diameter, and a series of metal rungs led to the top.

"Let's go up," Joe suggested. "And have a look around from a sniper's point of view."

Joe led the way. A few minutes later the brothers stood on the catwalk, looking down on the arena almost seventy feet below.

"Couldn't ask for a better place to shoot someone down there," Frank said.

"And the noise from the crowd would cover the sound of the shot," Joe pointed out. He stared down on the roof of the announcer's box and the bleachers below.

"We know it couldn't be Krieger," Frank said. "He was in the arena too soon after Buck was shot. But Loretta would have had plenty of time to climb back down and leave the rodeo grounds before the police got here."

"It doesn't look good for Loretta," Joe agreed reluctantly. "Maybe I'm wrong about her, Frank. Maybe Loretta did shoot Buck. Her marriage was on the rocks and she stood to inherit a bundle of money if Buck died."

"Exactly," said Frank. "She had motive and means. She's a trick shooter. We might as well go down. There's nothing else to see up here."

As Joe walked across the catwalk back toward the concrete support, he stopped abruptly and grabbed Frank's arm. "Look at this," he said, dropping to his knees."

"Mica," Frank said. "Just like that we saw in Loretta's trailer and on Matt's boots."

"This is crazy," Joe said. "There's a pattern here. This is the third time mica has shown up. It's got to mean something, Frank. It's *got* to."

"Let's go down and check out the base of the column again," Frank suggested.

Joe went first, climbing backward down the steel rungs. Then Frank lowered himself onto the rungs that led down the inside of the concrete support. He suddenly stopped.

"Look at this," he said, pointing to a small hole gouged into the cement. He stuck his finger in. "It's at least three inches deep," he said.

Five feet below his shoes, Joe was examining the cement wall on the left side of the rungs.

"Frank! There are bits of mica all over the wall here. And scuff marks."

Joe descended the rungs another five feet and stopped to study the wall again. "And here!" he said excitedly. "Like someone was walking up and down these walls."

"This looks like someone pounded a spike in here." Frank twisted his head to peer down at Joe, who had raised his head to Frank.

"You mean someone drove a—what did Matt call it—a piton into the cement and hung a rope from it," Joe said.

"Rappelling," Frank said. "Just the way mountain climbers lower themselves down vertical cliffs or rock faces."

"The only faster way to the ground would be to fall!" Joe exclaimed. "The sniper could have been down off this catwalk in fifteen seconds or less."

The Hardys descended the rest of the way, examining the cement wall carefully. A trail of mica and scuff marks led all the way down.

"So I guess we can put Kid Clown back on our list of suspects," Joe said when they reached the ground.

Frank still needed convincing. "We need a motive," he said. "And as far as suspects go, maybe we should keep Matt on the list, too. He's the one with mica all over his boots."

Joe was surprised. "Do you think he—" Then he stopped. He knew Frank was right. Every angle had to be examined. "Another alibi to check out," he said.

Frank nodded. "And we've got to get over to Matt's office now. We're already late."

As Frank and Joe walked from the arena to the back of the dance hall, the Texas sun was flexing its muscles. Already the rodeo was coming to life. Ticket holders were starting to stream in the gates and fill up the best seats.

Matt Halloran was waiting for Frank and Joe with Hank and Boone. Both men had deeply tanned skin with weathered creases from years of tough outdoor work.

"Matt told us what you want to ask us," Hank said before either Frank or Joe had time to say anything. He was chewing on a toothpick, and it bobbed up and down in the corner of his mouth as he spoke. "The truth is, we was standing with Rodeo Rick right when Buck was shot."

"That's right," Boone seconded. "Rick didn't want to watch Buck ride. And we were congratulating him on his score."

"Well, thanks for telling us," Joe said. "I guess that clears Rodeo Rick of the shooting."

There was a moment of awkward silence in the room before Boone spoke again.

"We been hearing rumors that it was Rick who salted Rocket's oats and let loose that bull the other day. Well, I ain't saying it is or it isn't.

But I'll tell you this. I've known Rick for years and he's not a bad man.''

"That's right," Hank said, moving the toothpick from one side of his mouth to the other. "He ain't the rider he used to be, and maybe that's made him do some things he shouldn't have."

Frank noticed Matt listening carefully to the cowhands' words. "I'll remember what you've said," Matt assured them. "Thanks for coming by."

The cowhands filed out as Matt turned his attention back to Frank and Joe.

"I have to get up to the announcer's booth before the opening event," he told them. He picked up a sheet of paper from his desk. "But I called a buddy of mine who was in early at the phone company and I have that information for you. It turns out there was only one call to the Flying B Ranch on the morning Buck was shot."

He handed the sheet of paper to Frank. "That's the number of the phone it came from. Apparently it's a cellular phone, and the local company doesn't keep a record of those numbers. You guys will have to check out who made the call."

With that, Matt left his office. Joe memorized the telephone number that Matt had jotted down.

"Let's call it," he suggested.

"Go for it," Frank said, gesturing toward the phone on Matt's desk.

Joe picked it up and quickly pushed the correct digits. On the other end of the line, he heard a telephone ring five times. He was just about to consider it unanswered when someone picked up and said hello.

Joe's eyes grew wide, and he swallowed.

"What is it?" Frank hissed.

"Er, Buck?" Joe asked finally. "Buck Fuller?"

The voice on the other end was so loud, Joe had to hold the receiver away from his ear. Even Frank could hear it.

"Who is this?" the voice demanded. "What do you want?"

"I think I have the wrong number," Joe said. "Sorry to bother you." He replaced the phone in its cradle.

Frank stared at Joe. "It couldn't be Buck Fuller, Joe. He's in a coma in the hospital."

Joe nodded slowly. "I know that, Frank. But it sounded like Buck." He paused, then added, "Or maybe his brother!"

Chapter

12

"WE BETTER FIND OUT whose phone that is right away," Frank said.

"Let's start here at the rodeo," Joe suggested.

The Hardys walked out of Matt's office into the reception area where Matt's secretary was typing.

"We were wondering if you have a directory of the telephones here at the rodeo grounds," Frank asked politely.

The secretary, a kindly-looking woman with an enormous upswept hairdo, stopped working. "Well, I can give you the main number for the rodeo, but there are about twenty extension numbers also," she said.

Joe shook his head. "We're trying to trace a cellular phone."

"In that case, it's probably in a car and belongs to a cowboy who drove here to compete." The woman reached into a desk drawer and took out a thick file of papers.

"All the cowboys camped here for the rodeo have to register and list their phone numbers. If it's here at the rodeo, it's supposed to be in this file." She handed the papers to Frank.

The Hardys went back into Matt's office and flipped through the papers as quickly as they could.

"I found it!" Frank said triumphantly, holding a registration form in his hand. "Joe, you're brilliant! Your hunch is paying off!"

"What?" Joe cried. "Show me."

Frank held out the registration form. The writing was sloppy and almost illegible, but the signature was clear. "Bruce Krieger," Frank announced. "Also known as Kid Clown."

"So that's who I was just talking to on the phone," Joe mused. "I couldn't believe how much he sounded like Buck Fuller."

"And that might also explain how Loretta was fooled," said Frank. "But I don't get it. What does Krieger have to gain by shooting Buck?"

"He was awfully interested in Buck's money," Joe pointed out. "Remember, after Buck was shot Krieger was telling us that if Buck died, and Loretta was convicted of his murder, she wouldn't inherit a cent."

"That's not a motive," Frank said. "But I do

think we have to walk over to Kid Clown's trailer and check it out."

As the Hardys left Matt's office, the rodeo was about to begin. As he passed the arena Frank heard a booming voice announcing the first event.

"I wonder if Aunt Gertrude and Mrs. Halloran made it over," said Frank, scanning the crowd on the chance he might see them.

"Probably," Joe said. "But you'll never find them in this crowd. Aunt Gertrude told me they're going to the dance again tonight and would like us to go, too."

The brothers jostled their way through the crowds to reach the campgrounds.

"There's Krieger's trailer," Joe said, pointing past a row of RVs to a battered pickup truck parked beside a trailer. On the side of the trailer "Kid Clown" was painted in bright red, white, and blue.

They were fifteen yards away when the trailer door opened and Kid Clown stepped out, dressed in full makeup and clown regalia.

"Quick!" Frank said, grabbing Joe's arm and pulling him behind a nearby RV. "Don't let him see us. He must be on his way to the arena."

Frank peered around the edge of the RV and watched Krieger lock the trailer door and walk off toward the arena. When he was out of sight, Frank signaled Joe with a wave of his hand.

They sprinted over to Krieger's trailer. The

campground appeared to be deserted. Joe took out a pocketknife and poked the smallest blade into the lock. Carefully prodding and turning, he heard it click. Then he pushed against the door. It swung open and the Hardys went inside.

The trailer was small but comfortable enough for one person. There was a kitchenette with a propane stove, a small bathroom, a living area, and a bedroom with a made-up bed in it.

Frank and Joe split up, each checking a different room. Joe went through the kitchen, even looking in the small trash can that stood in a corner. "Nothing," he said when he was through.

Frank's luck wasn't any better. He pulled the pillows off the small couch in the living room and checked them over, then put them back exactly where they had been. He pawed through a laundry basket that contained nothing but soiled clothes. He spotted a cellular telephone on a table and lifted the receiver. The telephone number written under the buttons was the same as the number from the Dry Valley telephone company.

Joe knelt and checked under the bed, finding nothing. He spotted a set of drawers built into the wall and opened the drawers one by one and moved clothing aside. At the bottom of the top drawer, he spotted a thin brown envelope. A piece of paper was folded inside. Joe read, "Last Will and Testament of Buck Fuller."

"Frank," Joe called softly to his brother in the next room. Frank poked his head in the open doorway. "Look at this. How did it end up in Krieger's trailer?"

"Wow!" Frank exclaimed. "I think we just discovered who ransacked Buck's RV."

Joe nodded. "That's what he was searching for and he found it. But why?"

"Open it," Frank instructed.

Joe unfolded the document. He gave a low whistle. "I guess those rodeo prizes really do add up," he said. "According to this, Buck is a very rich man. And he's dividing everything between Loretta and a children's charity."

"If Buck dies, and Loretta is convicted of murder," Frank pointed out, "the charity gets everything then."

Joe shook his head. "Wrong, Frank. Because there's no will anymore. Krieger's got it. So if Buck dies without a will, and his wife is in jail, then what happens to his money?"

Frank shrugged. "In most states, it would go to the nearest living relative, and if there are no relatives, it goes to the government."

"Let's see what else we can find." Frank scanned the tiny bedroom and spotted a narrow closet door in the wall beside the dresser.

"Did you look in here yet?" he asked Joe, reaching out and opening the door.

"Jackpot!" Joe called out when he saw what was inside.

"I'll say," Frank stated quietly. He gazed down at a pair of scuffed climbing boots that glittered with mica. A long coil of thick nylon rope lay beside them along with several steel pitons.

"Looks like Krieger's been doing some mountain climbing out at Sparkle Bluff," Joe said.

"And inside that shaft over at the arena," Frank added. "With Loretta's rifle in his hands. Joe, I think this case is closed."

Suddenly Frank and Joe heard the trailer door slam open. They spun around to see Kid Clown standing in the doorway. Even through his clown makeup, Frank could read the surprise on his face.

Before Frank or Joe could move, Krieger reached inside his bulky overalls and pulled out a snub-nosed .38 revolver.

"Make a move and you're dead!" the clown snarled.

Leveling the gun at Frank and Joe, Krieger pulled the trailer door shut and stepped all the way inside.

"Maybe you two aren't quite as bright as everybody around here thinks," Krieger said, leering though his painted smile. "I leave my trailer for a few minutes and look what I catch—two junior-size detectives."

"Matt Halloran knows where we are," Frank bluffed. "If we don't show up to meet him, he'll come here for us."

Krieger threw his head back and started to laugh. "Nice try, kid, but I know for a fact Halloran doesn't know where you are. Why do you think I came racing back here? I had a feeling you might be nosing around because I overheard Matt tell Terri Garcia about the videotape you watched last night."

"What video?" Joe pretended to know nothing about it.

"Don't play innocent with me," Krieger growled. "Seems your little old aunt taped Buck's shooting, and Halloran told Terri you two were all excited about it. I figured it might show me arriving a little late and coming from the announcer's booth. Good thing I put two and two together and hustled over here to catch you in the act."

Krieger glanced quickly around the interior of the little trailer, spotting the open closet door and the brown envelope, which was still in Joe's hand.

"Toss that over here," he ordered. Joe threw the envelope on the floor.

Krieger retrieved it, keeping his eyes—and the gun—aimed at the Hardys. "I should have burned this right away," he muttered.

"I don't know what your game is, Krieger," Frank said. "But we can prove you shot Buck and framed Loretta."

Krieger laughed again. "The game is money," he snarled. "Once Buck is dead and Loretta's

123

convicted, under Texas law I stand to inherit everything—with no will.''

Frank and Joe stared at Krieger as if he were crazy. Joe remembered the phone call he'd made to Krieger's trailer earlier that morning. And for the first time, Krieger was speaking to both of them in a normal tone of voice, instead of using Kid Clown's. It was unbelievable how much his normal voice sounded like Buck Fuller's.

"You're Buck's brother, aren't you," Joe said quietly.

Krieger's eyes opened wider. "Maybe you're not as dumb as I thought." He snickered. "Yep, that's right. That detective Buck hired tracked me down to an Oklahoma penitentiary where I was doing time for armed robbery. He came on the same day I was due to be released. When he told me who my brother was, I figured I found me a way to make some easy money. Once Buck was dead, that is.''

"You killed that private detective, too, didn't you?" Frank shot out.

"Right again, bright boy," Krieger responded. "Got him out of the picture before he could tell Buck about me. Then I got this little gig together as a rodeo clown.''

He chuckled cruelly, moving slowly toward the kitchen counter. Without taking his eyes off the Hardys, he reached into a drawer and took out a thick roll of heavy tape. He tossed it to Frank.

"Start tying up your kid brother," he ordered. Frank exchanged a quick look with Joe. Krieger spoke again, his voice forceful and cold. "Don't try anything. I'm faster on the trigger than you are on your feet. And when I shoot, I shoot to kill. Now, tie him up and fast."

Reluctantly, Frank picked up the tape. "Sorry, Joe," he said quietly.

Krieger stood back and watched as Frank wrapped tape around Joe's wrists and then around his ankles. As Frank worked, Krieger proudly revealed his scheme.

"When Buck and Loretta split up a few months ago, I figured I was on easy street. I just had to wait for the divorce before knocking Buck off. But then the two of them started talking about getting back together again."

"So you decided to frame Loretta," Frank said.

"That's right," Krieger boasted. "I called her, pretending I was Buck. Then I stole the rifle from her trailer, went up on the catwalk, and shot Buck. I rappelled down from the catwalk and was back in the arena in no time. As soon as I was finished there, and before the police had time to investigate, I got my rappelling equipment out of the tower and put the rifle back in Loretta's trailer. Everything went real smooth."

He jabbed the gun at Frank and Joe. "Until you two showed up. I figured you were getting a little too close to the truth yesterday. That's why I sent that hay wagon after you. Too bad it missed."

"What are you going to do with us?" Joe asked, sitting with his back against the wall, his hands and feet bound with tape. Frank stood beside him, his eyes riveted on Krieger, waiting for any opportunity to turn the tables on his captor.

"Same thing I did to that detective," said Krieger, leering evilly. "A little car accident will take care of everything."

Frank watched Krieger point the gun at him and reach into the kitchen drawer again. This time he took out a roll of fine, thin wire.

"You, lie down on the floor beside your brother," Krieger ordered Frank. "I don't expect tape will hold a couple of bright city-boy detectives like you two, so I keep a little piano wire on hand for emergencies like this."

His clown smile grew even broader. "I hope you try to pull yourselves loose. See, this wire will cut through flesh and bone like a knife if you put pressure on it. But don't take my word for it—give it a try."

Lying facedown on the floor, Frank felt Krieger wrap the wire around his wrists. Then his ankles were bound together. Krieger finally moved to Frank's head and slipped a wire noose around his neck.

"This'll keep you from rolling around," Krieger said, tying the noose to the wires that bound

Frank's ankles. "Unless you want to choke yourself. Or cut your head off."

After Frank was bound, he watched Krieger move to Joe and tie wire over the tape. "You'll never get away with this," he said angrily.

"That's what you think," his captor growled. Krieger disappeared momentarily, and Frank heard the sound of fabric ripping. Then he was back.

"You two talk too much," he snarled, bending down and tying a cloth gag over Frank's mouth. Then he gagged Joe as well.

When he was finished, the brothers were lying on their stomachs on the floor. All Frank could see were the bulbous toes of Krieger's big clown shoes on the floor in front of him.

"Now all I got to do is get that video your aunt took, and I'll be in the clear," Krieger crowed. "I called the hospital today. Buck's still in a coma. It'll be easy to slip in there and finish him off. After Loretta's in jail, I'll come forward and claim the money."

Frank became aware of Krieger bending over him, checking the wire around his wrists and ankles. Already the wire was biting into his skin. His face was drenched with sweat, and his muscles were screaming. He felt Krieger search through his pockets to get the keys to the red sedan.

"Nice of Matt to let you guys have the use of

his car. I bet he never figured it would be a death vehicle for the Hardy boys.''

Frank heard the keys jangle as Krieger tossed them in the air. The door of the trailer opened, and he blinked against the sudden glare of bright sunlight streaming in from outside.

Krieger laughed fiendishly. ''Kid Clown's got to get back to work,'' he said. ''But as soon as it's dark, I'll be back to take you two for your last ride!''

Chapter

13

FRANK LAY PERFECTLY STILL on the hard floor of the trailer, with the piano wire pressing into the flesh of his wrists, ankles, and neck. Even the slightest movement of his legs pulled on the wire that connected his ankles and neck, tightening it like a noose and threatening to strangle him.

He felt the trailer heating up as the hot Texas sun beat down on the metal roof. Sweat trickled down his face, tickling him and stinging his eyes. One hour, then two, crept by, but he dared not move.

On the floor next to him, Joe tested his bonds. Since Krieger had wrapped the piano wire over the adhesive tape, his wrists and ankles were protected from cuts. But the wire around his neck dug into his skin, growing tight unless he kept his legs perfectly still.

Joe tried to speak, but it was impossible. The gag was too effective, and all that came out was muffled gibberish. After what seemed like an eternity, Joe decided to grit his teeth against the pain and make a move.

Keeping his body as stiff as possible to avoid tightening the piano wire, he began slowly rocking from side to side on his stomach, each repetition of the move a bit stronger. When he thought he had enough momentum, he tucked his shoulders and rolled over on his back. Sweat—or blood—seeped from under the wire around his throat, but he'd done what he set out to do, and the pain was worth it.

Joe had long ago become fluent in Morse code, the alphabet system of dots and dashes once used by telegraph operators. Now, thought Joe, it might save their lives. Slowly he tapped his index finger against the floor, spelling out a message.

"Knife in left shirt pocket."

Hearing the tap, tap, tap of Joe's finger on the trailer floor, Frank forgot about the heat and pain, and focused his attention on his brother's message. In his position he was unable to respond—but he understood instantly what Joe was driving at.

Joe rolled onto his side, and slowly, fractions of an inch at a time, wriggled closer to his brother to make it easier for Frank to reach into his pocket. Minutes crept by, the heat in the trailer stifling.

Gasping for air, Joe slowly positioned himself so his breast pocket was level with Frank's hands. Steeling himself against the pain, Frank began to move onto his side. Trickles of sweat on his face tormented him, and his eyes burned. Finally his fingers rubbed against the fabric of Joe's shirt, and his thumb hooked on the pocket flap.

Frank felt the wire digging cruelly into his neck and cutting off his air. He kept his breathing slow and shallow. The wire around his wrists was so tight that his fingers were numb and could barely move. Black circles began to spin in front of his eyes, and he knew he was close to passing out.

Frank began to move his numb fingers slowly and rhythmically, to get the blood to flow into them. His fingertips tingled painfully, but he welcomed the sensation. He eased his fingers into Joe's breast pocket.

The sound of footsteps outside the trailer brought instant fear, and Frank's heart pounded. Then the footsteps moved on. Frank breathed a sigh of relief and forced himself to relax. Then he went back to work. After what seemed like an eternity, his fingers closed gently over the handle of Joe's pocketknife.

Moving with infinite slowness, Frank drew the

knife forward until it was half out of the pocket flap. He let go, and it fell the rest of the way, landing on the floor with a soft thump.

Joe felt the knife being released from his pocket. Carefully he rolled away from Frank, and lay on his back again. "Good," he tapped in Morse code on the floor. He waited patiently, until his heart stopped pounding and he'd adjusted to the renewed tightness of the piano wire pressing into the flesh of his neck. Then he rolled again, so that he was facing away from Frank.

He shook the sweat from his eyes, and glanced at the window in the door. Although the heat in the trailer was still suffocating, the sun was beginning its western descent. It had taken them hours just to get the knife out. Krieger might be back any minute. As he thought about this, Joe could hear the distant roar of cheers from the arena.

Joe groped behind him until his fingers touched the cool handle of the knife and closed around it. He maneuvered it between his palms, then sought the indentation of the blade with one of his fingers. It took many tries before he could get the blade partly open. When he did, he wanted to whoop with joy.

He heard footsteps going past the trailer again, and voices. Contestants had begun to return from the arena. From a distance, a man's voice called, "Bruce, how about a little poker tonight?"

Joe heard Kid Clown answer with a loud honk

from his horn box. "Not tonight," Krieger called back in his silly, high-pitched clown voice.

With a sinking feeling, Joe realized it was too late. Gritting his teeth as the wire pressed deeply into the skin of his neck, he forced himself to roll over, and wriggled back toward Frank. The open knife was clenched tightly between his fingers.

Frank heard Krieger's voice, too, and felt a cold chill sweep his body, despite the heat and stale air in the trailer. A key rattled in the door lock. Frank felt Joe press against him again, thrusting the open pocketknife into his rear pants pocket.

Kid Clown opened the door and stepped into the trailer. No light came in with him—a heavy cloud cover must have moved in.

"You big shots miss me?" Krieger snickered. "Sorry I had to leave you alone so long. I promise it won't happen again. In fact, after another hour or so, nothing will ever happen to you again."

Frank heard the ripping sound of adhesive tape being unwound. Krieger's foot came down on his shoulder, and with a kick, Frank was rolled over on his stomach. His body screamed with pain from his bonds.

"I'm going to have to retie you guys," Krieger said. "Wire doesn't burn, and your corpses would be found all wired up. But this here tape burns away real nice. After your little car accident, the car is going to burst into flames. If the crash doesn't kill you, the fire will. Fire has a nice way of covering up murder.''

Half unconscious from lack of oxygen, Frank was only dimly aware of Krieger standing over him. He felt the man's hands grab his wrists, and cold metal pliers cut the piano wire. Quickly Krieger replaced the wire with layers of strong adhesive tape. He moved on to Frank's feet, releasing the wire that connected them to the loop around his neck. Frank gasped for air, filling his lungs.

Joe watched Krieger work on Frank's bonds before turning to him. The killer leaned over Joe, smelling of sweat and greasy makeup. Quickly he snipped the piano wire binding Joe's limbs, then checked the adhesive tape to make sure it was still tight.

"Almost party time, guys," Krieger taunted. Frank heard him leave the trailer and slam the door behind him. The light in the trailer was dim. It was twilight now and the clouds obliterated what little light was left. Outside, the engine of Krieger's pickup truck started up.

Joe began to wriggle across the floor toward Frank again, angling so that his hands would be able to retrieve the knife. Without the wire bounds, he was able to move faster and with less pain.

Aware of Joe's movement, Frank listened to

the sounds outside the trailer. He heard the pickup truck slip into gear, and the sound of the engine grew louder. He guessed that Krieger was backing it up to the door of the trailer. Unable to speak through his gag, Frank groaned urgently to warn Joe to move back.

Joe heard Frank's grunts and stopped. The door handle rattled, and quickly Frank pushed himself back to where Krieger had left him a few moments earlier.

"I saw your red sedan over in the parking lot behind the dance hall," Krieger said, reaching down and grabbing Frank under the arms. He started dragging him across the floor to the door. "Thought I'd take you over in the pickup truck, so no one over here will see me messing around with Matt's car."

Frank felt himself dragged out the door and over the tailgate of the pickup. A moment later Joe was lying beside him. A smelly canvas tarp was thrown over the brothers, and the pickup started to rumble out of the campground.

It was a short ride to the parking lot behind the dance hall. Krieger threw back the tarpaulin and stood over Frank and Joe. He reached down and dragged Joe to the end of the tailgate. Joe saw the red sedan beside the pickup, the rear door open. Krieger walked around and crawled inside the sedan. Then he reached over and dragged Joe roughly inside. Soon, Frank was lying on the floor beside his brother.

Krieger slid into the driver's seat and threw a heavy object into the back. The pungent odor of gasoline filled the car.

"I ain't going to leave nothing to chance," he said. "Maybe the car will catch fire on its own after the crash, but I want to make sure. Got your marshmallows, boys?"

He started the car and drove slowly out of the parking area. "I'll have to hitchhike back after you boys have your accident," Krieger told them. "But I figure every step will mean another few hundred dollars for me. Buck must have better than a quarter of a million or so in the bank— and it's all going to be mine."

He laughed so hard he began to cough. "I won't have any hard feelings after this is over, even though you two tried to send me back to jail. In fact, every time I light a cigar from now on, I'll think of you!"

Joe and Frank bounced around on the floor of the backseat as Krieger drove away from the rodeo grounds. After a while the car rumbled onto rough gravel, and they heard the engine strain as the car climbed a long, winding road. Outside, the night was pitch-black, but stars were beginning to shine through as the clouds slid away.

"Not much traffic here near Sparkle Bluff at night," Krieger said. "Everything's working out real nice for me."

The tires screeched as Krieger took a turn too

fast. "I guess I better slow down," he said. "I don't want to have an accident on the way to the accident." He laughed at the cruel joke but slowed down considerably.

In minutes the climb had become so steep the car's transmission was wailing. Suddenly they ground to a halt. Frank heard the engine die and then felt Krieger's hands roughly pulling him into the driver's seat. Joe was pushed into the passenger seat. Then Krieger grabbed a gas can from the backseat and splashed it around the interior of the car.

Propping himself up, Frank gazed through the windshield. The ink black sky was filled with stars. They were parked on a rocky bluff. Barely visible, probably thirty feet away, the mountain ended in what appeared to be a sheer drop.

"It'll look like you city slickers got lost and made a real bad turn," Krieger laughed. "I'll tell your aunt goodbye for you when I get that videotape from her."

Stooping through the open door, Krieger reached past Frank and shifted the gear level into neutral. He slammed the door, walked to the rear of the car, and started pushing. It didn't take much to get the sedan moving. Krieger laughed crazily. The car picked up speed and rolled toward the deadly precipice.

"So long, guys!" he shouted as the red sedan moved toward the edge.

Chapter

14

THE MOMENT Krieger slammed the door of the sedan shut, Frank was getting the knife out of his back pocket.

Joe was sprawled across the passenger seat, his head slumped against Frank's shoulder. His arms were pinned behind his back and taped securely. His nerves and muscles screamed as he pulled uselessly at his bonds.

The car moved slowly at first. Frank heard Krieger grunt with effort as he got the car moving. The sedan picked up speed, bit by bit, heading toward its inevitable catastrophe. The reek of gasoline was almost overpowering.

Frank felt the open blade with the fingers of both hands, and pulled it halfway out of his back pocket. He started rubbing the tape binding his wrists against the sharp edge. He bore down hard, not caring that the knife was already biting into his flesh.

The sedan gathered speed, its tires crunching stones and scrub brush. Frank's wrists broke apart, the tape still clinging to both wrists. With one hand he grabbed for the door handle, with the other he gripped Joe securely by the arm.

There was a slight bump as the front wheels of the car moved over the edge of the precipice. The front nosedived violently then, and through the windshield Frank watched stars in the night sky blur fast. A blast of chill air hit the car as the door swung open. Frank threw all his weight to his left, hurtling himself and Joe out of the car. They slammed against rocks while the car continued its aimless descent, bashing against rocks and boulders as it fell.

In the sudden silence Frank became aware that he was lying on his side on a narrow ledge ten feet below the top of the bluff. His body ached. Joe was breathing hard beside him. Suddenly he saw the dark figure of Kid Clown silhouetted at the top of the precipice. Frank froze.

A loud explosion from far below split the night air. An orange glow moved up the side of the canyon and flickered against Krieger's face. "Bon voyage, boys!" he called down into the chasm.

Frank listened to the clown's laughter and the sound of his footsteps fading into the darkness.

From the depths below, the flames of the burning car shot up.

Frank pushed away from Joe and felt for the knife. It had survived the fall. He pulled it out of his pocket and cut the gag from his mouth.

"Be right with you, Joe," he said, slicing the tape from his ankles. His mouth was dry from hours with a rag stuffed in it. He moved over to Joe's side and cut away the gag.

"Not a second too soon," Joe mumbled, ripping the gag away. Frank cut the tape from his brother's hands and ankles. Joe peered over the ledge at the car burning far below.

"That's one ride I definitely didn't want to take," he said.

Frank was examining the narrow ledge that had saved their lives. It was only five feet wide, and the top of the cliff was well over his head. There were lots of scrabble holds, but a mistake meant death on the rocks below. His wrists and ankles hurt painfully, and hours of being in bondage had numbed his hands and feet.

"It's a good ten feet back up to the top," Joe said. He moved to Frank's side, rubbing his arms to restore the circulation. "Give me a boost and I can drag myself up the rest of the way. Then I'll reach an arm down for you."

"Let's go!" Frank said. "We need to get to Aunt Gertrude before Krieger does."

"Ready?" Frank asked. He clasped his hands

and held them under the pointed toes of Joe's western boots. He hefted upward.

Joe rose up the cliff, with Frank pushing him from below. His hands grabbed into the rock at the top of the bluff, and he scrambled over.

On the ledge below, Frank eyed a thin crevice that angled up the face of the rock. Using it for a foothold, he began to climb, pressed against the rock until he felt Joe's hand touch his. The brothers' hands clenched together. Joe pulled with all his strength until Frank slowly appeared over the lip. They rested a moment, panting from the exertion. Krieger was nowhere to be seen. Moonlight now bathed the desolate bluff and the dry dirt road that led down the mountain.

"Let's get to the Double X," Joe said.

Frank and Joe started jogging along the road, alternating their gait between speed-walking and running to conserve their energy. The road was dark and lonely, and wound downhill for several miles. At the bottom of the mountain, the lights of isolated ranches twinkled far in the distance.

"Maybe we can find a farmhouse and phone the Double X," Joe suggested.

"I have a better idea," Frank said. He gestured behind them. Still a long way off, but approaching steadily, were the headlights of a vehicle. "Let's hitch."

A few minutes later a four-by-four pickup bore down on them. They waved frantically from the middle of the road, and the truck ground to a halt. Frank ran to the driver's window. The driver was an elderly rancher. He listened to Frank's story of a car accident with suspicion until Frank mentioned that their destination was the Double X Ranch.

"Y'all a friend of Matt Halloran?" the crusty cowboy asked. "Why sure, get in the back of the truck. This road comes out on the interstate right near the Double X."

Frank and Joe drove across the flat moonlit fields of Texas in the back of the pickup, the wind whipping their hair. The countryside was almost completely deserted, with rangeland stretching to the horizon. Almost an hour later the sky ahead of them glowed, and they saw traffic sweeping along the interstate.

The driver let them out at the driveway of the Double X. Frank and Joe started up the road on foot.

"Something's wrong," Frank stated flatly as they approached the big brick house. All the windows were ablaze with light. He started running, Joe right after him. When they reached the yard, they stayed in the shadows of the cottonwood trees and slowly circled until they were underneath the living room window.

Frank slowly rose on his tiptoes and peered inside. The room had been torn to pieces!

"Krieger's been here," he said to Joe. "And I don't like it. It's too quiet."

"You take the front door," Joe proposed. "I'll take the back."

The brothers split up. When Joe reached the backyard, he saw the door wide open, banging against the side of the house. Carefully, he moved forward, pressing against the brick wall. When he came to the door frame, he peered around it into the kitchen.

The room was empty, silent, and the scene of frenzied destruction. Everything had been ripped from cupboards and smashed on the floor. Joe slipped into the house, glancing quickly into the laundry room and the dining room as he moved toward the front.

Frank was in the front hall when Joe got there. He shook his head wordlessly to indicate he had found nothing. Joe picked up the telephone on the hall table. It was dead.

"He's cut the line," Joe said softly. "We can't even call the police."

"Let's check upstairs," Frank suggested. He bounded up the stairs, Joe right behind him. The bedrooms were in a similar condition to the rest of the house. Krieger had spared no effort in his search for the videotape.

"By now Aunt Gertrude's at the big dance with the Hallorans," Joe said when they were certain the house was empty.

"And I bet she has her camcorder with her," said Frank.

"Right. With the videotape still in it." Joe

143

looked at Frank. "I bet Krieger's figured that out by now, too. We better move."

They raced to the front door. Frank saw the lights of the rodeo glittering across fields half a mile away. A light breeze carried the faint sounds of country music from the big dance hall.

He grabbed Joe. "There are horses in the barn. We can get there a lot faster that way."

The brothers ran across the grass toward the barn behind the house and entered it through the side door. Six horses were contentedly chewing hay in their stalls. Each wore a halter. Frank stopped and unbuckled his belt.

"We can use these as reins," he instructed Joe, ripping it from the waist of his pants. "We don't have time to saddle them."

Joe threaded his belt through the halter of a white horse, and swung onto its back. Frank chose a bay. Joe clutched the belt and bent low over the horse's mane. Without a saddle and stirrups, he found himself gripping the horse tightly with his legs. He dug his heels into the horse's sides, urging it to run faster.

The horses were fresh and strong and set off at a gallop that was smooth and easy. Together, Frank and Joe tore across the fields toward the rodeo.

When Frank reached the edge of the rodeo grounds, he slowed his mount to a halt. Joe pulled up beside him on the white horse. Fifty yards to their right, the rows of RVs and trailers were quiet. On their left, rows of cinder block stalls were lit by naked light bulbs. A dirt track led among pens of horses and bulls, with chutes leading to the arena several hundred feet ahead of them.

"Let's tie up the horses and go the rest of the way on foot," Frank suggested. "Krieger could be anywhere, and he still has that thirty-eight."

"Good idea," said Joe. "Up on these horses we're easy targets."

They dismounted and tethered the horses to the steel fence that formed a pen around several mean-looking bulls. Suddenly Frank heard a pop. A geyser of dust kicked up at his feet.

"Duck!" Frank shouted. "Someone's got a gun and is shooting at us!"

Chapter

15

FRANK LOOKED AROUND desperately for cover. There was none, except a pen filled with bulls and another that contained a small herd of broncos.

A slug buzzed by Joe's head as he crouched beside Frank. Another slug *pinged* off a steel gate. The bulls inside the pen started milling about, snorting wildly. On the other side, a bronco whinnied loudly and reared up on its hind legs, its forelegs flailing the air. Several more shots hissed through the night, clearing Frank and Joe's heads by inches.

"I got more bullets than you got time!" Krieger yelled. "I ain't going to quit until you're both dead."

Frank and Joe cringed close to the ground.

Joe glanced around, peering through the moonlit night for any sign of Bruce Krieger. He spotted a thick coil of rope hanging around a post on the metal gate beside him. He reached up and closed his hand around it, quickly plucking it off the fence.

Frank stared at him quizzically.

"You never know when you might need it," Joe whispered, tying a long loop in one end. Terri Garcia had taught him well. He put his arm through the coil and rested it on his shoulder.

"Give up, Krieger!" Frank shouted. "You'll never make it!"

He listened for an answer, but heard only the troubled snorts of bulls and the restless hooves of the broncos. Drifting out on a warm gentle wind, the sounds of country music and a square dance caller came from the dance hall.

"He's up to something," Frank muttered to Joe. "I can feel it."

"Hey, I'm the one with the hunches," Joe whispered. "By the way, that's my hunch, too."

"Let's untie the horses and get ready to break out of here fast," Frank told Joe.

The brothers moved toward their horses. Keeping low, they untied the belts that held the animals to the fence.

Joe spun around at the sound of hinges squeaking loudly. "There he is, Frank!" he cried, spotting a dark shadow run between the pens. He heard one of the metal gates opening.

147

"He's letting the animals out!" said Frank, suddenly alarmed.

Krieger fired three rapid shots over the pens, whipping the animals into a panic. A bull bellowed and charged through the open gate onto the trail, two more bulls behind it. In the other pen, the broncos reared up, their hooves coming down hard on the steel fence. The horses charged through the gate, and ran into the herd of stampeding bulls.

"Let's get out of here!" Joe yelled, jumping up and racing for his horse.

Frank leapt onto the bay's back, just as the first of the bulls charged at him. Then he saw a horse and rider on the far side of the bronco pen.

"There's Krieger!" Frank shouted. "He's getting away!"

Joe dug his heels into the side of his horse and slapped the horse's flank with his hand. It sprang forward, galloping down the track toward the arena. Frank rode beside him, the panicked animals stampeding only a few feet behind them.

Ahead of them, Joe saw that the pens ended. Only a single fence separated them from the road that ran around the arena. Krieger's horse was twenty feet ahead, on the other side of the pens.

Joe urged his horse on, straight at the fence, and wrapped his arms around the beast's thick neck. The horse arced over the fence. Seconds after he came down on the other side, Frank's horse landed beside him.

Joe saw Krieger straight ahead, now with a fifty-foot lead. The killer glanced back over his shoulder before he turned his horse toward the road that led to the rodeo entrance and highway.

"He's trying to get away," Joe screamed.

Frank quickly realized that he could make it to the road faster than Krieger if he went across a grassy picnic area.

"I'll cut him off!" Frank shouted, leading his horse to outflank the escaping criminal.

Frank's horse galloped forward, leaping over a picnic table and closing in on the road. Krieger looked back just as Frank reached the road. He reined in his horse so hard the animal reared back. Frank watched as Krieger pulled up sharply and turned his horse in the opposite direction. The clown dug his heels into the horse's flanks, and the animal took off at full gallop—straight for the open doors of the dance hall!

Joe swung around the corner of the arena and saw Krieger change direction. He looked ahead. The entrance of the dance hall was crowded with cowboys—probably drawn outside by the sounds of the stampeding animals. Joe urged his horse forward and gained on

Krieger, narrowing the distance between them to less than ten feet.

He saw the dance hall coming closer and closer. The faces of the people gathered at the entrance suddenly filled with terror at the sight of the on-coming horsemen. They started to scatter as the horses pounded forward.

Joe shrugged the coiled rope down his arm and grabbed it just before the loop. He started swinging it, letting the rope out bit by bit. He swung harder and harder until he could hear it hum around his head.

Krieger tore through the entrance of the dance hall on his horse. Screams interrupted the sounds of music and merriment, and dancers fled from the dance floor, racing for safety at the side of the room.

Joe went in the dance hall right behind Krieger. He spotted another open entrance at the side of the hall at the same time Krieger did.

Putting all his strength into a throw, Joe let the loop sail through the air ahead of him. The forward momentum of the loop drew the rest of the rope through Joe's hand and settled down over Krieger's head and shoulders. Krieger's horse kept going. Joe reined in, clenching the rope. The loop tightened around Krieger, pulling him off his horse. The rodeo clown landed hard on the polished hardwood floor.

Joe swung down off his mount and raced to Krieger's side just as Frank tore into the hall.

Dancers started to mill around them, their faces stunned.

Matt Halloran pushed his way through the crowd. "What the—" he started.

Joe interrupted. He waved his hand at Krieger, who was still sprawled on the floor. "Loretta is innocent," he announced loudly. "This is the guy who shot Buck."

"And we can prove it!" Frank Hardy said, moving to Joe's side.

Matt stood with his hands on his hips. "Where have you guys been all day? Your aunt Gertrude and I have been worried about you two."

A slight grin playing across his face, Joe said, "We were tied up all day. So to speak."

Frank nodded. "Then we had a little moonlight ride."

"Yeah," Joe added. "Right over a cliff."

Terri Garcia stepped out from behind Matt. "That was a great rope throw," she said, staring at him with astonishment. "You learned real fast, Joe."

Joe pointed at Krieger. "Frank and I always get our man," he said proudly, flashing her a smile.

The crowd that had gathered around the boys suddenly parted. Aunt Gertrude strode into the center, her camcorder held tightly to her eye. She panned Frank and Joe, sweeping the camera past them to focus on Bruce Krieger.

"I thought you two were going to stay out of trouble on this vacation," she told them.

Joe smiled. "Come on, Aunt Gertrude," he said. "If it wasn't for Frank and me getting involved, your travelogue wouldn't even have a storyline."

A few days later Matt stood on a platform at one end of the arena. Dry Valley Rodeo's closing day ceremonies were beginning. The bleachers were filled to capacity, and all the competitors were lined up across the arena.

Frank and Joe Hardy stood next to Matt, and beside Joe was Terri Garcia. His piece of rope handiwork had impressed her. Suddenly Joe was getting a lot more attention from the trick roper.

"Thanks to Frank and Joe Hardy," Matt began, speaking into a microphone. "The Dry Valley Rodeo has been a big success—and Bruce Krieger is behind bars."

Applause rang out through the arena, along with whoops and cheers.

"Now someone you all know is going to make a special announcement," Matt said. He stepped aside, and Loretta Fuller walked up to the mike. Being out of jail had done her a world of good, Frank thought. She glowed with happiness.

"Here's the best news of all," Loretta told the crowd, tears in her eyes. "Buck woke up from his coma this morning! His doctors say he's going to be fine!"

Frank nudged Joe. "A happy ending," he whispered. "Like all cowboy stories should have."

Joe smiled at his brother. "Better than happy, Frank," he said quietly.

Frank looked at him. "What do you mean?" he asked, puzzled.

Then he saw Terri Garcia reach out to take Joe's hand. Joe looked back at Frank, his eyes glowing.

"We got the criminal"—Joe's blue eyes twinkled—"but I get the girl."

Frank and Joe's next case:

Vanessa Bender has received a rude welcome to Bayport High—her car tires have been slashed in the school parking lot. But the Hardy boys learn that vandalism is the least of the new girl's worries. Vanessa's mother has just opened an animation studio, and her plan to unleash a collection of crazy cartoon canines on prime-time television has set off a deadly chain of events.

A fire at the studio and the death of one of the show's creators may send the entire production up in smoke. But Frank and Joe soon bring the big picture into focus. It's a clear case of arson . . . and murder. Using the art of illusion, the boys hope to draw the culprit out of hiding. The plan has only one flaw— the killer has already drawn a bead on them . . . in *Mayhem in Motion*, Case #69 in The Hardy Boys Casefiles™.